ABOVE THE CIRCLE OF THE MOON

The Cornishe Chronicles: Book 1

T.M. TUCKER

23 Digital Ltd

Dedicated to Aileen Tucker for her love,
wisdom and inspiration.

"Presumption is our natural and original infirmity. Of all creatures, man is the most miserable and frail, and therewithal the proudest and disdainfulest. Who perceiveth and seeth himself placed here amidst the filth and mire of the world, fast tied and nailed to the worst, most senseless, and drooping part of the world, in the vilest corner of the house, and farthest from heavens'-cope, with those creatures that are the worst of the three conditions. And yet dareth imaginarily place himself above the circle of the moon and reduce heaven under his feet. It is through the vanity of the same imagination that he dare equal himself to God, that he ascribeth divine conditions unto himself, that he selecteth and separateth himself from out the rank of other creatures. To which his fellow-brethren and compeers, he cuts out and shareth their parts and allotteth them what portions of means or forces he thinks good. How knoweth he by the virtue of his understanding the inward and secret motions of beasts? By what comparison from them to us doth he conclude the brutishness he ascribeth unto them?"

An Apology of Raymond Sebond, by Michel Eyquem de Montaigne, translated by John Florio

❧　I　❧

12th March 1766, Savanna la Mar, Jamaica

"Dogs, that's what we are. Nothing but dogs."

Cyrus the mulatto was speaking to Plato the slave. It was close to midday and the sun was punishing this part of the island and all who trod on it. Both Cyrus and Plato had errands to run, but they weren't urgent. The morning had already ground to a halt, and Cyrus sat in the main square, taking a short rest to conserve energy for later in the day, when his real labour would begin. He reflected on the lot of the slaves in the fields. A painful time for them, this. It was harvest, and the slaves had little relief from the heat and toil. The trade in sugar waited for no man.

"Dogs," said Cyrus again.

Plato turned and gave him a lazy stare. "What?"

Cyrus nodded to the centre of the square. There was a small, sandy-coloured mongrel staggering around in the heat of the morning. Its legs were stiff and moved in random jerks. Its head twitched, ears flat, tail spinning around in wayward circles. A few feet from the dog stood a stout white man: a farmer, judging by his clothing. He was deeply engrossed in conversation with a man of similar stature and appearance, and was paying no mind to his pet.

"But you are a free man," said Plato.

Cyrus ignored the remark. He knew he was relatively privileged. After all, he was the son of Joseph Cornishe, the white plantation overseer from whom he inherited his icy blue eyes. But he had the smooth brown skin and rich black hair of his mother, the slave girl only ever known as Lucy, and it was this that was destined to define him. In any case, he hated his father, and his father hated him. That's why he'd sent him away. Ostensibly, it was to learn a trade, but Cyrus knew that what Joseph Cornishe really wanted was to be rid of his mixed-race son. And so he'd ended up here in Savanna la Mar, apprentice to a carpenter. At the age of twenty-one he was all set up for a semi-skilled profession, on a par with blacksmiths, shoemakers and tailors. In the future he could expect a reasonable living, with a similar income to a sailor or a fisherman. But he could never aspire to a position higher than that.

Cyrus nudged Plato's arm. "See there? That dog is free. He has no leash; he can run away any time he wants. He could easily outrun his master right now, and would never be caught."

Plato shrugged.

"But if he ran, he'd be captured or shot or beaten," Cyrus continued, warming to his subject. "There is nowhere for that dog to go. He must stay near his master or die. What kind of freedom is it, where you have nowhere to go?" A fly settled on Cyrus's arm. He didn't bother to brush it off. "He has no leash, but he may as well be tied to his master with a chain."

"Ain't nobody free in the eyes of the Lord," said Plato.

Cyrus turned to him with a look of disdain. "My friend, it will do you no good to listen to the Christian."

Plato stared at him now. "You sayin' there ain't no God?"

"There may be a God. But He is certainly not as the Christians describe Him. Just look at their works." Cyrus gestured around the square. European-style buildings clustered around this part of town, jostling for prominence with palm trees and traders' awnings. "Trade, slavery, buccaneering. What God would have it so?"

"Do you dare to question your Father?" came a hoarse voice from behind them.

Cyrus turned around to discover a shambolic white man glaring at him. He wore dirty blue breeches and a ragged white shirt. His hair was tousled and his face was red, most likely caused by excessive drinking rather than exposure to the sun.

"It is not God who enslaves you, it's the devil!" barked the red-faced evangelist, ensuring he could be heard by anyone within earshot. "Since Adam's primal disobedience, all mankind has been a slave to the forces of evil. The only way out of your prison of sin is to open your hearts to God's grace. Your soul is imprisoned in the dungeon of your flesh. You must find your way to the City of God to avoid eternal damnation. Only God will show you the way."

Cyrus snorted. "Put away your Augustine and pick up your Voltaire," he said, turning his head away from the zealot.

The preacher's face darkened. Cyrus noticed that Plato was shifting uncomfortably beside him.

"It is Calvin that shows us the way," the preacher replied, slurring his words somewhat. "And that French bastard Voltaire is a corruptor of our times."

"I see no difference between Calvin, Augustine or any other Christian thinker," said Cyrus. "They are the true sinners. The self is divided, yes, but not by God or the devil. It is society that separates us."

"What are you doing?" hissed Plato under his breath.

The dog across the square was diverted by the commotion, and pricked up its ears to identify the source of the shouting. It stopped its insane circling and focused its attention on the loud and violent man who was now gesticulating with both arms, as if fighting off demons. With a low growl, the dog darted towards the Calvinist and sank its teeth into his calf muscle.

"Argh," yelled the preacher. "Get this beast off me!"

He shook his leg, but the dog had a strong grip. The commotion alerted the farmer, who hurried over to pull his pet away from its victim.

"You'll pay for this," said the preacher. "I'll shoot the mutt myself."

"The beast makes a distinction," said Cyrus. "Are we not told that against the sons of Israel, a dog will not even bark?"

"Damn the children of Israel." The preacher was sweating profusely, and there was a light foam around his lips.

"We have to leave," said Plato. "We cannot stay here."

"Why not?" said Cyrus. "This is a public place."

"I ain't ready for the lash, that's all."

By now the dog's owner had managed to wrench the dog free of the preacher's leg, leaving an angry wound that oozed thick blood. The preacher fell upon the ground, rubbing the gash and proclaiming that the devil himself had taken possession of the hound.

"This is a good working dog," said the farmer. "He's troubled by your manner, that's all."

"I am a man of God!" shouted the preacher.

"Come," said Cyrus, taking Plato by the arm and moving off into a side street.

"Tsk," said Plato as they hurried out of the square. "You nearly get us killed."

They dodged through the back streets of Savanna la Mar. Slaves and servants shambled on their errands and chores. Shopkeepers sat in the shade, fanning themselves. White merchants gathered together in small groups here and there to discuss news from abroad and the politics of the day.

"You know, these are changing times," said Cyrus. "Look around you. The white men are outnumbered by negroes here. Ten to one."

Plato turned his head. "Yes, but they got the weapons," he snapped.

"You don't think we have weapons? Look at the tools they give us: knives, shovels, saws, axes. If it can cut through sugar cane and wood, it can cut through people."

Plato shook his head. "You heard what happen in Tacky's Rebellion? I knew some of them people. Do you know what they did to them?"

"Tacky came close," said Cyrus. "We will be more prepared next time."

"Hmm," said Plato. "You think maybe the Maroons will have better fortune."

Cyrus stopped walking and stared at him. "The Maroons? What about the Maroons?" He had barely finished his sentence when a tug at his collar yanked him to the ground.

"Is this the one?" A large white man in dirty white work shirt, grubby black shoes and a broad-brimmed hat stood over him.

"That's him," said the preacher, who was waddling to catch up with them. "The mongrel half-caste. Hold him still! I'll have him beaten for insolence."

"Run," Cyrus hissed to Plato. "And tell Tom Hartnell what is happening here."

Plato bolted down the street without looking back.

"It's the cells for you," said his captor.

❧ 2 ❧

12th March 1766, Montego Bay, Jamaica

To Dr Melchior Croll, Bristol, England
    From Captain James Maddern

It feels as if I have been gone from Bristol for so long that I am starting to lose any sense of the civilisation I left behind, though in truth it cannot be much more than three months since I departed.

As promised, I'm writing to keep you in touch with my progress. I landed in Hispaniola and made my way to Cap-Haïtien, where I began my enquiries into the occult happenings there, just as we discussed. I began immediately to follow up on the rumours of the voodoo ceremonies that you'd told me about. With the money you gave me to offer as incentive, I soon found slaves that were willing to talk, although they were highly fearful of being discovered. Through these contacts, I discovered a branch of voodoo that is referred to here as *Don Pedro*. This cult is well established and seems to have come over with the Africans, as far as I can tell, although it has been embellished by the mixture of cultures in this new land. The details of the cult and its ceremonies were hard to extract from those I talked to, but after much pressing and bribery, I managed to persuade some negroes to take me to one of their secret gatherings and witness it for myself. I must tell you of this in detail – below is my full account of what happened.

I was led by two guides, both of whom were known and trusted by the *Don Pedro* leaders. They took me on horseback way beyond the town and into the countryside, off the main highway and along a winding bridle-path that led up into the mountains. They'd made it clear to me that I was taking a risk. If I were discovered, I could well lose my life. To avoid this, they blacked my face and dressed me in rough clothes, with a large hood to hide my face. You may well imagine my anxiety.

After the long ride we arrived at a rough wooden hut hidden among the trees, invisible to anyone who didn't know of its existence, so far was it from the main thoroughfare of human activity. Two large negroes guarding the door questioned each person before allowing them in. I was advised to draw my hood over my face and, as we came close to the gate-keepers, they stared at me with fierce expressions. They were about to ask me to remove my hood, when one of my guides gave a signal, a combination of hand and eye gestures that must have had some significance for the men at the door. After a pause during which my heart rose into my throat, they ushered the three of us through without further question.

Inside we found ourselves in a large room crowded with negro men and women of all ages. At the back of the room were two wooden thrones draped in blood-red cloth, on each of which sat a man and a woman, regal and proud, both adorned in long golden gowns. I stood with my two guides at the edge of the gathering, near the outer walls and close to the exit. They whispered to me that these figures were the *Papaloi* and *Mamanloi*, the priest and priestess of the voodoo order. Before the thrones stood a large wooden trunk. They told me this contained a snake worshiped by the *Don Pedro* priests.

A low murmuring hummed around the hut, which was silenced by a loud wail from the *Papaloi*. The high priest then signalled to a pair of drummers in the corner, who beat out a sinister rhythm. The *Papaloi* chanted in a language I did not recognise. This was echoed by the entire congregation, and to my intense discomfort I was forced to join in, for fear of being discovered. For some ten or fifteen minutes the murderous chant continued, all the bodies in the room now swaying to its deathly rhythm, while a large bowl was passed around for all to drink from. When it arrived at my person, one of my guides explained it contained an intoxicating mixture of liquor and mind-altering herbs, and I would be best not to ingest it if I wanted to observe the proceedings with any degree of clarity. I feigned drinking from it to avoid swallowing any of the poison, but a tiny amount of the foul-smelling mixture settled on my lips and I tasted something of its intense power.

The chanting continued and during the next twenty minutes I noticed a palpable change in the participants. They began to wail and holler and gyrate their bodies along to the incantation, bringing a dark, sexually charged atmosphere to the proceedings. Meanwhile, the priest intoned in broken English (the common language here), how if they were to be rewarded with bodily and spiritual health, they must do as the holy snake directed, whatever its desire. Some responded with positive shouts of obeisance and affirmations of their worship. As the chanting continued, the congregation became intoxicated by the combination of the drink and the ceremony, soon reaching a delirious fervour. The attendants exhibited a lunatic intensity of which I had never seen the like. Some went berserk, falling to the ground and wriggling like snakes, or climbing the walls and hissing in homage to the snake spirit.

The *Papaloi* gave out a great shout to stop the chant. The room fell silent. Many were swaying on the spot now, some with their eyes closed. I myself felt drunk and giddy, the result, perhaps, of the hellish atmosphere, and possibly the tiny amount of potion that had settled on my lips. Everything appeared distant and unreal, like watching a theatre piece from somewhere in the upper circle. Moonlight shone through the windows, glowing like the phosphorous algae I'd seen in the lagoons nearby. I was gazing upon this scene in a state of horrified awe, when my attention was drawn back to the thrones of the priests.

From behind the curtain two negroes emerged, bearing between them a young black boy child, maybe eight years old. The boy prostrated himself in front of the *Papaloi* and *Mamanloi* and gave assurance that he would do the bidding of the holy serpent. Clearly, he had been given precise directions for this ceremony and was following orders. But I sensed a hesitation in him, as if he wasn't aware of what might happen next.

The two negroes who had brought in the boy took him by the shoulders and laid him on the ground. One of them picked him up by his feet and lifted him into the air so that he was held suspended upside down before the audience. The other brought forward a brass bowl and placed it under the boy's head. At this point the boy started to scream in terror, as it became apparent to him that his life was in danger. The second negro produced from nowhere a long knife, like the kind used to cut sugar cane and, with a wild, whipping motion, sliced through the boy's throat. I am ashamed to say I let out a loud, involuntary gasp as the boy's blood spurted out in great arcs across the interior of the hut and flowed into the receptacle below him, whilst the two negroes clamped hold of his legs as he twitched.

Those in the crowd, who had clearly expected this development, turned to look at me. I felt the pressure of suspicion and an unconquerable urge to flee. I barged my way through the crowd towards the single door that led to the open air. As soon as I was outside of that hot and claustrophobic hut, I fell to my knees and vomited. I lifted my eyes to the heavens, and the full moon stared back at me as if to accuse me of complicity in these heinous sins. 'You were there and you didn't stop it. You could have saved that boy.'

I jumped on my horse, making the greatest haste to be away from that infernal hut. When I arrived back at my quarters in Cap-Haïtien, I went straight for my stock of rum, gulping the fiery liquid down, as if by drinking I would vanquish the memory. As the rum calmed my nerves, I began to regret my decision to run. I had come closer to fulfilling my mission. Perhaps I'd missed my chance to witness the supernatural power which we seek. But then I tracked back through my memory of the evening, and reassured myself there was nothing about the ceremony that showed any evidence of the supernatural. The great mass of people there had behaved as if possessed by demons, but that could be easily explained by the drugged liquid that had been passed around, and the communal spirit of the assembly.

The next day I went to find the guides who had taken me there, and what they told me only increased my certainty that I'd done the right thing by leaving when I did. The boy had been bled to death, cut into pieces and cooked up for the congregation to eat. I admit, I had been prepared for darkness, but this was much worse than I anticipated.

Nevertheless, my guides could report no evidence of black magic. The rituals, the sacrifice, the chanting and the fervour – none of it led to any supernatural events. The perpetrators of this horrible crime were murderous madmen, but not practitioners of any dark arts, as far as I can tell. Which means that I have yet to find evidence of the secret that I am dedicated to finding for you.

I have more to tell, but the recounting of these events has left me emotionally spent. In brief, I picked up on a promising rumour. From three different sources I gleaned reports of vicious attacks in Jamaica that cannot be explained. I'm told these attacks bear all the hallmarks of the *Jé Rouge*, as it's known here. I set off at the earliest opportunity, and I'm now in Montego Bay, in the north of the island. I will send this letter on the next packet boat, and write another when I have more news on these reports.

Perhaps soon I will have something to bring back to you, and I can return to Bristol with our prize. And then, God willing, and with your help, I will be reunited with my beloved Claire.

Until then, I remain your loyal servant,

Captain James Maddern

3

Cyrus was chained to the wall by an ankle bracelet. His cell was a tiny room with four stone walls and a heavy wooden door. Five other slaves were crammed into a space that would barely accommodate two of them lying down. They all sat with their backs to the wall and their knees at their chests, cramped together in the stifling heat.

Flies buzzed around their heads, but no one had the energy to shoo them away. It had been five hours since Cyrus had been captured and thrown in here, and he'd heard nothing in that time. Had Plato managed to get to Hartnell? If so, why wasn't he here, organising his release? Perhaps Hartnell was delaying in order to teach Cyrus a lesson. He'd done this before, as a way of venting his exasperation at Cyrus's wilder misdemeanours. It had been some time since the last such episode though, and Cyrus's behaviour had been good for over six months now. Hartnell would surely know the dangers of leaving him in the town gaol for too long. People lost their lives in these places.

Cyrus stood and banged on the wooden door. "I need to speak to my master," he demanded.

Nothing.

"Your master ain't going to save you now," said one of the negroes sitting on the floor, a bright-eyed young man of the Akan tribe with a scarred face and proud features.

Cyrus ignored him and battered the door again, louder this time.

"Why expect the white man to save you?" said the Akan. "Only black man can save black man."

"He not even black man," said another prisoner, a Coromantee from the Gold Coast.

"He blacker than white," said the Akan, smiling now.

Cyrus turned to face him. "Better I get out than stay in, whatever way I can, no?" he said. "I can't fight if I'm in prison."

The Akan's smile broadened and he gazed on him, as if searching his face for clues. "Are you a fighter, friend?"

Cyrus thought about answering, but knew he had to be careful. He'd heard how slaves were planted in places like this, offered special favours to weed out troublemakers. It had been six years since Tacky's Rebellion, but memories of that insurrection remained fresh for many whites on the island and paranoia ran deep.

The Akan looked away. "No matter," he said. "The Maroons, they be coming."

Cyrus stiffened. It was the second time this day he'd heard tales of the Maroons. "What do you mean?"

The Akan shrugged. "They are ready. Hundreds of them."

"Quiet," said the Coromantee, nodding at Cyrus. "You don't know who this be. Most probably a spy for the whites."

"I'm on your side," said Cyrus, straightening his shoulders.

"How you know what side I'm on?"

"The whites, they—" Cyrus began.

"Ain't you the son of a white man?" the Coromantee interrupted.

"I'm the son of a black woman," Cyrus replied.

The Coromantee jumped to his feet and thrust his face inches from Cyrus's. "No black woman choose to be with white man. You the son of a rapist."

Cyrus struck out, knocking the Coromantee back against the floor of the cell, where he landed in a heap on top of the other prisoners. There followed angry shouts from those who'd been disturbed and soon everyone in the room was agitated. Only the Akan sat still, his smile lingering. The shouts in the cell grew louder and more heated, until a slamming on the door from outside silenced them.

"What's going on in there?" came an angry voice from beyond the door. "Keep quiet, you black bastards, or you'll all be in the stocks before you know what's happening."

"I will not go in the stocks for this white man's bastard," said the Coromantee.

Cyrus swung a kick towards him but missed, and caught one of the other slaves with the edge of his foot. The shouting started up again, louder this time.

The door burst open and Cyrus felt himself struck in the back, which thrust him towards the back of the cell. He turned to see a white gaoler swinging a wooden club that caught the head of the negro nearest the doorway with a sickening crunch.

"Hey, hey," Cyrus bellowed. "Leave these men alone."

The gaoler swung his club towards Cyrus, but he was slow and Cyrus caught the man's arm to stop him swinging again. A thunderous shadow passed over the gaoler's face. "You're a dead man," he spat, pushing Cyrus's arm away with his other hand.

"No he ain't."

The voice came from the doorway, which now framed a professional-looking white man in bright blue jacket, cotton pantaloons and tousled hair. This man looked in his thirties, although his strong, pleasant features portrayed a wisdom beyond his years.

"Who the fuck are you?" asked the gaoler.

"Tom Hartnell," said the man in a broad cockney accent. "I'm here for my apprentice. Goes by the name Cyrus. Surname Cornishe."

The gaoler regarded Cyrus with regret now he wouldn't get a chance to beat the miscreant.

"I'll pay the fine," said Hartnell. "And then Cyrus comes with me."

The gaoler scowled and strode out of the cell, slamming it behind him.

Cyrus lifted his chin and looked around, but none of the negroes caught his eye, except the Akan, who beckoned him closer with a nod of his head. Cyrus leant down to acknowledge him.

"Speak to Harold. Shark's Head. He'll tell you."

Cyrus nodded and puffed out his chest as he stood tall. Within minutes, the gaoler returned and he was shown from the cell.

"You've got some explaining to do," said Hartnell, as he marched him from the gaol.

❦ 4 ❦

14th March 1766, Montego Bay, Jamaica

To Dr Melchior Croll, Bristol, England
      From Captain James Maddern

I have much of interest to tell you. My stay here in Montego Bay has been eventful, and it is leading to quite a breakthrough in our fortunes.

As soon as I got here, I set about looking for lodgings. After a few enquiries, I was directed to the guesthouse of one John Tallway, a retired plantation overseer who runs a property at the edge of town. I took a small offshore bag with me and resolved to stay a few nights while I made enquiries about the rumours surrounding the *Jé Rouge* here in Jamaica. On my arrival, I was greeted by a striking young black girl named Rose. I judge her to be around twenty years of age, but her looks immediately struck me as so cold and bitter that it gave me the strong impression she had seen much of life in that time.

Rose showed me to the mistress of the house, Mrs Tallway. She led me upstairs to a small, sparsely furnished room that seemed perfect for my needs, and came at a reasonable price. I paid Mrs Tallway upfront for three nights. She must have been impressed with my purse, because next she offered me the 'use' of Rose. I think you can guess what was meant by the phrase. I'm sure you also know that I have no desire for intimacy with any other, apart from my dear departed Claire, and I declined of course. Mrs Tallway merely nodded and suggested that if I changed my mind, I need only say so.

I took a light rest on the bed that afternoon and awoke with sweat clinging to my skin. It was an early evening heat that seemed to me even hotter than the heat of the day. I suspect the accumulation of the sun's intense activity must have settled into the walls and floors of this dark little place. I dressed myself and went to explore the streets of the town around Montego Bay in search of supper. As I descended the stairs I passed an older gentleman, a fellow lodger I presumed, opening the door to an adjacent room. Standing with him was the girl, Rose. I only glanced at them, but I guessed that Mrs Tallway had successfully sold the use of the girl that evening. I confess I felt a small sadness for her. No doubt that look of weariness I had spotted in her face earlier was due to the life she had been forced to lead. And who knows what misery that might lead to for a young girl?

I dined out reasonably well in a local inn and thought no more of the incident. Until I returned to my lodgings. I was in my room, preparing for a much-needed sleep, when I heard disturbing sounds from the gentleman's room. There were heavy male grunting noises, followed by the sound of one human being striking another, and a yelp, undoubtedly from the female. Then more striking, followed by outright screaming, so high pitched and fearful that it stiffened my veins to hear it. I leapt from my bed, heart racing. As I hesitated, there was a short pause, and then all hell broke loose. Furniture crashed against the wall that separated my room from theirs, accompanied by screams from the girl, and gruff shouts from the gentleman. I dashed into the hall to find Mrs Tallway standing ashen faced on the stairway, yet unwilling to take the step of interfering with the matter. Cursing her, I hammered on the door.

"Fuck off," came a drunken shout from within.

I could not be a passive bystander in this situation, and after tugging at the door handle, I put my shoulder into it and slammed into the door. Mrs Tallway begged me to restrain myself, but after two hefty barges the door flew inward. Rose was lying at the brute's feet. Her clothes were ripped and her face gashed and bruised. The man, who was clearly anything but a gentleman, had his tights around his ankles, and was brandishing a broken bottle, the jagged shards of which were stained with dark blood. He was snarling with rage, as if possessed by the hounds of hell.

"How dare you intrude on my personal affairs," he bellowed, baring yellowed teeth.

I stepped between the girl and her attacker and glared into his angry, drink-sodden eyes. "Enough," I said.

This confrontation appeared to confuse him. He stared at me dumbfounded, long enough for the girl to pick herself up and scamper through the door to safety. I turned to see her bump into Mrs Tallway, who grabbed her and tried to push her back in. I was stunned and told the landlady in no uncertain terms to let the girl go, which, after a minor hesitation, she did.

"Get back to your business, Mrs Tallway, I'll deal with this," I said.

She was clearly nonplussed by my peremptory tone, but she submitted and left the scene almost as quickly as Rose. I turned back to the man who faced me.

"Sit down, sir."

He looked at me with devilish insolence.

"Sit down, I say, or you will regret it!"

He was heavier than I, fat around the stomach, but considerably shorter, and older by ten years or more. He sized me up with a glower, and then sat on the side of his bed, the bottle slipping from his grasp onto the floor.

"She would not do as I told her," he said, like a child telling on his sibling.

"It is abhorrent to inflict violence on a girl of such a young age."

At this he snarled again. "She's a goddamned slave, man."

"Slave or not, it is hardly the Christian thing to do."

This seemed to move him, and I saw something like embarrassment in him as he averted his eyes from mine.

"I suggest you get some sleep," I told him.

He snorted and then did just that, flopping down onto his bed. By the time I got to the door and closed it behind me, I could hear his snores.

I peered down the stairway, listening out for any activity. I could hear Mrs Tallway's admonishments. I leaned over the balcony to see her standing outside the girl's room and berating her through the closed door.

"Mrs Tallway, I would like to get some sleep, if you please."

She looked up at me and back to the doorway, then sucked her teeth and turned to go back to her own room. I stood for a few minutes to make sure that the scene had died down, then returned to my room.

This in itself, while eventful, would have not been worth remarking on if it weren't for what transpired the next morning.

I was awoken by a devilish commotion. Shouts, yelps and cries resounded as if they were in my own room. I sprang from my bed and into the hallway, only to discover that Mr and Mrs Tallway were arguing in the neighbouring room, standing over the prone body of the gentleman, laid out across his bed in the same position as I'd left him the night before. Mrs Tallway was hysterical, but I discerned from her husband that the man was dead. I checked his breathing and pulse and confirmed it. There were no obvious wounds or signs of violent behaviour.

"It is the girl, she is wicked," said Mrs Tallway. "Her Obeah magic, that's what it is."

At the mention of the Obeah, my ears pricked up. "What are you suggesting, Mrs Tallway?"

Mr Tallway spoke for her. "This girl is known for her practice of that dark art." He looked ashamed, and then almost whispered as an aside, "It is one of the reasons why we employed her here."

"But the man has not been moved," I said. "It is likely that he died from alcohol consumption."

"No, I have seen this before," Mr Tallway replied. "The Obeah have the power to take the life of one who has wronged them. It is the girl, I tell you. I will deal with her myself." He turned to leave, and I was quite sure he was ready to drag her out of her room and beat her to death. But I sensed an opportunity and called to him.

"Mr Tallway, it would not do for you to punish the girl here. You already have one death on your hands; you surely don't want the reputation of two corpses in the same day."

This gave him pause, and I used this to improvise a rationale.

"Is this girl owned by you?"

"Yes," he said. "We bought her from the church just this month."

"The church?"

"Yes, they found her troublesome. They had hoped to cure her of her Obeah worship. I think they are glad to be rid of her."

"Listen," I said. "I am good friends with the governor here. In fact, I'm on my way to see him. Let me take the girl to him and explain the situation. That way she will get the justice she deserves, and your lodging house will suffer no more from the scandal. I will pay you the correct rate for her."

Mr Tallway paused to think about this. "I can make more from whoring her out than we do from the lodging rates."

"A reasonable plan," I said. "But is that working out for you? From her behaviour, I can see she might be more trouble than you'd hoped for."

He looked me up and down, as if for the first time assessing my standing. I could see he was calculating his options and, after a short time of reflection, he nodded agreement. "Twenty pounds."

My shock must have been evident. "I can buy three slave girls for this price in the market."

"As I said, I had expectations of revenue from her. This will make up some of my loss, at least until I find another to replace her."

"I can give you fifteen pounds."

"Seventeen."

"Done."

We shook hands.

"What about the body?" he asked, nodding towards the corpse on the bed.

"I will alert the town doctor. He'll need to deliver a diagnosis on the cause of death and other particulars before passing on this terrible news to his kin. In the meantime, do you have somewhere we can store it?"

With some difficulty, Tallway and I manoeuvred the deceased rogue into an empty storeroom at the back of the house, and laid him out on the cold stone floor. This was hardly the most dignified resting place, but I had no reservations with this particular man.

Next it was time to talk to the girl. I knocked on her door and made my most reassuring appeal.

"My dear, there will be no harm done to you. I believe you're innocent and I merely wish to establish the facts."

She did not respond, so I spent a good deal of time trying to convince her. Finally, I reasoned thus: "You must come with me, girl. The only alternative is for us to force the door down and physically restrain you. I'm sure you don't want that."

The door swung open. She stared at me, her chin tilted up. I stepped inside so that I could speak to her privately.

"Listen," I whispered. "I mean to make an agreement with you, one that will be beneficial to us both. But first I need to understand. Is it true that you are a practitioner of the Obeah form of witchcraft?"

Her left eyebrow twitched but she said nothing and maintained my gaze.

"I will take that as a 'yes'. Now, did you kill this man?"

"What if I did?"

"I'm not going to punish you. In fact, I need your help. There is something on this island, something supernatural, that I must discover. It is my understanding that those who practice Obeah have the ability to discern such things. If you're willing to travel with me and help me find it, I will help you evade prosecution. If all goes to plan, I may even be able to offer you your freedom."

She gave the slightest of smiles. "I ain't never going to be free," she said. "Ain't no one can give me that."

"I will do my best, of that I assure you. As I see it, this is the best of all options for you."

In short, I left with Rose that afternoon. Once we were free of the house, I took her to a local inn to eat. I suspect it was her first good meal for quite some time. I think she saw that she could trust me, and after a little probing I got her to admit that she had killed her attacker with the power of Obeah. It seems she had been mentored for some time in these dark arts by an elderly woman who took her under her wing when her parents were killed during a foiled rebellion.

Rose has six years' experience in the arts and is quite adept. More to our purpose, she has a specific gift for divination. She claims to be able to 'see' through the eyes of supernatural creatures – ghosts, demons, witches, shape-shifters. According to her, these exist on the same plane, that of the Obeah. She is able to lock onto that plane and inhabit their perspective.

I took her back to the Black Prince and gave her use of the quarters there. As I write, she sleeps soundly in the hold. In the morning I will start work with her to discover the nature and circumstances of that which we seek.

Tomorrow I will send this letter to be forwarded on the next packet boat to you. I'll continue to send you updates as they occur. I consider it a journal of my adventure. At present, I have nowhere for you to send return letters. As soon as I find a place to settle, I will let you know.

Until then, I remain your loyal servant,

Captain James Maddern

14th March 1766, Savanna la Mar, Jamaica

Tom Hartnell stood in the centre of the room, a candle illuminating his face from below. His tousled hair glowed in the light of the flame, giving it the appearance of a judge's wig.

"I got distracted," said Cyrus.

"You're always distracted. What was it this time?"

"A mad preacher in the square. He attacked me."

"Attacked you?"

"I mean, verbally attacked me. A dog bit him, and I was blamed."

"Hmm," said Hartnell.

"There were witnesses. Ask Plato."

"It's not the first time, is it? Your father has spared nothing to give you a leg up in life. And then he's paid me to have you trained as an apprentice carpenter. You know he didn't need to do any of that, don't you? You're a half-caste. You don't have the same rights as whites."

"Well, I wish he didn't want rid of me, but he does," said Cyrus.

"Is that what you think? That he wants to be rid of you? My boy, if only you knew of your father's real motives."

"I'm sure I could never guess his real motives. We're hardly of the same mind, are we?"

Hartnell placed the candle on a nearby table and scanned the room. Cyrus's bed, little more than a heap of dirty blankets, lay in the corner. Next to it was a pile of books. He leant forward and picked up three of the volumes, turning them over to inspect them in more detail. *Leviathan* by Thomas Hobbes. *Lettres Philosophique* by Voltaire. *A Treatise of Human Nature* by David Hume.

"Tell me, Cyrus, how exactly are these helping you become a better carpenter?"

"They're helping me become a better person."

Hartnell tutted, shook his head. "They're filling your head with ideas, that's what they're doing."

"And what is it about 'ideas' that scares you, exactly?"

Hartnell sighed. "I'm not afraid of ideas, Cyrus. But I'm a practical man. And I'm being asked to train you to be the same. These," he threw the books on the floor, "these *distractions* can only slow that training down. The only book you need to become a good person is the Good Book."

Cyrus pursed his lips. "I'm afraid I have yet to find anything in there that's of any use to me."

"Perhaps you aren't looking hard enough." Hartnell picked up the other books from the pile besides Cyrus's bed. Locke, Johnson, Descartes. He placed them on the table next to the candle.

"I think some time without these will help."

Cyrus's eyes widened. "My father gave me those. You can't take them away."

"Well, I'm sure he's pleased you've read them, but he wants you to learn to be a carpenter, and eventually, a man of your own means. When you're free to practise your own business, you can read whatever you like. Until then, focus on what I'm teaching you. And nothing else."

"But it's part of my education. My father would insist."

"I'm talking to your father at the weekend. We'll see what he says about it then. In the meantime, I'll bring you the Bible. There's plenty to read in there."

Cyrus scowled but he knew further protestation would have no effect on Hartnell. The man was as stubborn as hammered iron.

"And for Christ's sake, no more lateness. From now on, I want you back here as soon as you've done your duties." With that Tom Hartnell turned and left the room, carrying the confiscated books with him.

Cyrus fell onto his bed and cursed. Another of his freedoms curtailed. And this the most important. He knew well that real liberation came from the expansion of the mind. Hume and Voltaire had taught him that much of what appeared to be true was a deception, and that things could be otherwise if we chose to see them that way. It gave him courage to imagine a different future for himself.

He closed his eyes and tried hard to recall his favourite passages from Voltaire's *Candide*, a work that had hit him with particular force. But he was tired and the words wouldn't come. Only the sense of excitement that freedom would bring. He felt it like a force, as if the pressure of his will would break real chains as easily as a piece of string. While he let this feeling envelop him, he noticed the sounds of the town beyond his walls. Shouts of drunkards spilling out of nearby inns. The movement of people, horses, the wind. Laughter and shrieks. All of life itself was out there and he could not participate. He was back on the leash. He'd be given leave on certain occasions; get issued tickets, as many slaves did, to go on errands for their masters; granted free passage for a limited period. But he could still be stopped at random by any white man and challenged on his precise activities.

Now his mind turned to the news that the Akan had given him in the gaol. Were the Maroons about to wage war against the British?

The Maroons. The very mention of them struck fear into the hearts of the whites. Yet this small army of unconquered blacks, descended from the freed slaves of the Spanish settlers, fascinated Cyrus. When the British took over the governance of Jamaica in 1655 the Spaniards were banished, but their ex-slaves retreated to the mountains, where they formed a stronghold. But two regiments of regular troops, the entire militia of the island, and even the wild buccaneers employed by the British, all failed to defeat them.

Under the legendary leader, Cudjoe, and the Obeah influence he established, they unified into a fearsome force. Cyrus had heard how they ambushed white invaders in the passes of the so-called Cockpits of Jamaica, inaccessible highlands furrowed by gaps and ravines, which formed perfect traps for any would-be aggressors. They took arms and ammunition from those they defeated, picked off anyone who approached their land, and the British military authorities declared they were more difficult to defeat than any army in Europe. Both sides were depleted by the fighting over many years, and eventually the British persuaded these fearsome guerrillas to sign a treaty. The Maroons gained assurance of their freedom, in return for allowing the whites open roads through their territories. And what had always pained Cyrus: they gave a promise that they would apprehend and return any black slaves that escaped from the British plantations and tried to join them.

But now he'd heard from two different sources that they were preparing to rebel again. This could be the revolution he'd been waiting for. The moment was surely ripe for a true overturning of white society. He wanted more than anything to be part of this, to be present at the start of the new collective. He must find a way to join the Maroons. Maybe he could offer them something they needed. He had much knowledge of Black Castle, his father's estate, knowledge that no outsider could possibly possess. This could be useful to them. There were enough downtrodden slaves who had suffered on the estate, and their number was sufficient to overcome the white men who ran it. All they needed was direction and leadership. They didn't like or trust Cyrus, but if he came to them with a plan, and a fighting force of Maroons, they would have to listen.

But what of his father? Certainly Cyrus could not protect Joseph Cornishe. The man was the overseer of Black Castle Estate; he was as guilty of the white men's crimes as anyone. True, he lacked the cruelty that other owners bestowed on their slaves and servants, and was never sadistic like some of them. But he did punish slaves from time to time, and often without a second thought.

No, Joseph Cornishe would have to go the same way as any of the other white men who tried to stop the progress of this revolution. There was nothing of Joseph Cornishe that he wanted to save or protect. Hadn't the man already shown what he thought of Cyrus? He'd demonstrated a clear neglect of his duty as a father, sending him off to others for instruction and mentoring. What Hartnell said about his real motives was a lie. No doubt Cornishe would one day father a white child by a white mother, and that would end any residual concern for Cyrus. Why should Cyrus wait to discover his true fate? Why not act now and forge his own destiny?

Cyrus opened his eyes and looked up to the ceiling of mould and crumbling plaster. There was nothing left for him here, only subservience and neglect. He'd make the journey to the Maroons himself. He knew where they lived. Maroon Town and the nearby Cockpit Country was a day and a night away by foot, or so he'd heard. He could get there before Hartnell had time to alert his father to his disappearance. It would be a risk, without a ticket from his master, stating when he'd set out and when he was due to return, which the authorities required of all unaccompanied blacks. Perhaps he could get Hartnell to issue one for a minor excursion?

As Cyrus pondered these plans for uprising and freedom, he drifted into a deep sleep, and before long his snores could be heard throughout the carpenter's house.

❦ 6 ❧

16th March 1766, Montego Bay, Jamaica

To Dr Melchior Croll, Bristol, England
    From Captain James Maddern

Such strange occurrences have I experienced over the past days that I feel the need to write it down and send it to you. Allow me to resume my story from where my last letter ended.

After I'd brought Rose back to the Black Prince, I questioned her to find out how she can help us find the object of our search, which is rumoured to be on the island. For this she told me that she would need the help of her elder, the one who had trained her in the Obeah arts. This was new information, and my first suspicion was that she had lied about her abilities and was now stalling. Besides, even if it was true, I wasn't keen on bringing others into our affairs. The less people involved the better. But after some argument, during which she insisted that elder knowledge was crucial to our quest, I concurred. This meant travelling to the elder's living quarters, some ten miles out of Montego Bay. Fortunately, Rose can ride, so I bought two horses in town at a good price and we took the journey.

It was a revelation.

Her mentor is an old black lady, around sixty years of age, known only by the name of Obi. She lives in a shack in the forest and exists on the food she catches and gathers there. She is frail and thin, she dresses in dirty rags, but her face has a fierce power to it. And her eyes! By God, they are fixed and bright, so much so that I found it difficult to look at her directly. Despite her prominent bones and heavily wrinkled skin, she possesses an inner power that shines out of her.

With Rose's help, I consulted this witch about the nature of what we are seeking.

She affirmed to me that our object is on the island. "Been here," she said, pointing to the ground.

"You've seen it?" I asked, with some excitement.

"No, not seen. Felt. In spirit. There is Ashanti proverb: *Sasabonsam ko ayi a, osoe obayifo fi.* When Sasabonsam go attend funeral, he lodge at Obeah house.'"

"What is Sasabonsam?"

"Your word is 'devil', I think. Is word used by Ashanti for person possessed by spirit. The forests of Ashanti, and what white men call the Gold Coast, are where Sasabonsam live. Man see him covered with long hair and with feet that point both ways. Is known by priests and witch doctors in Ashanti. Many who enter them forest never found again."

"But how did you come to encounter it here?"

"Was many years ago. Something important to Sasabonsam died. I felt presence of devil spirit in my house. Is how I know him nearby here."

"This devil – what is its nature? Is it a man, or beast?"

"Both. There be many kind like this. In Africa, the Bouda people had power to change themselves into hyena. In kingdom of Kaffa, them called Qoras, who change into leopard, lion and shark. The witches of Makanga could become crocodile. Some of these can change at will, some at certain times, others need their potions and their rituals. I think this Sasabonsam is *Jé Rouge* – man-wolf. It can only come during three days of full moon each month."

This was part of our conversation, but I have half-filled a notebook on what else she told me, which I will preserve for your research. We later got around to talking about how we can find the creature. This is where Rose comes in. Her particular power is to see through the eyes of the spirit, without it being conscious of her presence. This way she may find clues as to what man or woman we are looking for. I am thinking it is likely a slave on one of these plantations, but there are thousands here. Finding this creature will be a challenge.

The old woman explained that for Rose to inhabit the spirit's mind, she must undergo rituals and incantations unique to the Obeah. The first step was to gather the right ingredients. I watched her carefully, as I knew that you'd appreciate some details on the procedure, but she worked quickly and it was often difficult to see exactly what she was doing. From what I could see, Obi and Rose sourced a variety of organic material – feathers, bones, eggshells, some inner organs of a fish and the skin of a small lizard. Rose explained that it was important to incorporate living things from land, sea and air into the concoction. The next step was to grind them all together. With this powder Obi mixed some foul-smelling liquids and what looked like dried blood from her store of dark materials.

Next came the ceremonial part of their work. The two of them sat together, closed their eyes and murmured incantations in front of a small fire that burned mauve and purple and sparked with unnatural brightness. They fell into a trance, their eyes closed, their bodies swaying, their voices humming. I felt a sudden sharp memory of the voodoo ceremonies I'd seen in Hispaniola, and with the smell of the potion and the insufferable heat, I had to get outside for air. By the time I returned I found that Rose was still in her trance, but the old witch was awake and sitting opposite her in front of the fire. As her guide, she took her hands and whispered instructions in another language, or so it seemed to me, and not one I'd recognised from my time in the West Indies. This went on for some time. I tried to focus but the nausea returned, and I wasn't making any sense of their communication, so I retreated outside and sat in the shade away from Obi's hut.

When I returned to the room Rose had come out of her trance. She took a moment to recover, before drinking from a revitalising tonic provided by the old woman. When she had fully composed herself, she told me of what she'd learned from her visions. It seems that she connected with the Sasabonsam while it was in human form, and was able to see through the demon's eyes. She could discern a rural setting, possibly a plantation, but she wasn't able to determine precisely where. However, she did sense it was under some kind of protection. Whether this was from other creatures, spells, incantations or some other force, she could not tell me. There were few other clues in her vision, but there was one thing of significance. She visualised seeing a name, possibly on a note or letter, that she felt would lead us to the demon. The name was Hartnell. She was certain he could be found somewhere in Savanna la Mar. As this was our only tangible clue, we will go next to enquire after anyone answering to that name.

Rose had to rest after her exertions. I spoke to the old woman and asked if there was anything more we could do, but she replied that there was nothing. The girl's powers were drained, and she would need some time to recover. I asked her how we would be sure we knew the creature when we encountered it. Just as you'd briefed me, she confirmed that we'll need weapons of silver if we hope to inflict any damage to the creature. Wounds from bullets or steel blades will do no long-term harm, whereas silver bullets or blades will kill if they penetrate a werewolf's heart or brain.

Leaving them, I took a walk in the forest. This whole experience has revealed to me more of my weakness and I felt a rush of confusion from the activities I'd witnessed. I stumbled across a dry streambed and followed its course, soon discovering a section with a deeper well of water. I lay down on my stomach on the bank, and reached my arms down to draw the water over my head in great cascades. It felt like a cleansing and soon my strength was revived. By the time I sat up and considered my surroundings, I understood the panic I was feeling was coming from a place of alienation and fear.

Oh Melchior, I feel so far from home and so desperately in need of familiar ground. You know I love to travel and explore, but the violence and mystery I've experienced through these few weeks in the West Indies is hard to bear. I am maintaining my focus, though, for the sake of you and ultimately for the sake of my beloved Claire. I confess to you now that I had never truly believed we might find a way to resurrect one whose life had been taken from her. I had always hoped, of course, because of the faith I put into you and your experiments. But now, after meeting Rose, and my encounter with Obi, I am starting to believe. This can be no conjuring trick, surely?

Nevertheless, I can't help wonder what price we are paying for this collusion with the supernatural. Must it be that we endure such horror and darkness to win back my love? I feel like Orpheus on his journey to the Underworld, seeking his beloved Eurydice. Is my fate, like his, to wander the remote wildness of modern-day Thrace? Even if I do survive, and Claire is brought back to me from beyond life itself, can my true love be a just reward for the indulgence of such evil?

Forgive me, Melchior, for these meandering doubts. I have a mind to tear up this letter and re-write it with nothing but the facts. But I have never hidden my thoughts from you, and I shall not begin now. I know that if I beheld you face to face, you would again convince me of the merit of our undertaking. Let me envisage that you sit with me here, in the oppressive heat of an alien landscape, accompanying me on this shared adventure. If this avenue of possibility is as promising as it seems, I will soon have what we require: a specimen of an immortal, that I can bring to you for your vital research. A research that may yield happiness, not just for myself and my beloved Claire, but for all the human race.

Until then, I remain your loyal servant,

Captain James Maddern

7

17th March 1766, Savanna la Mar, Jamaica

To Dr Melchior Croll, Bristol, England
    From Captain James Maddern

Rose and I left the Obeah witch and went back to Montego Bay to prepare for our trip to Savanna la Mar. I discovered a bladesmith in that town, with whom I discussed my need for silver weapons. He explained that there is little demand for such a thing, as silver is too soft for weaponry. However, he did happen to have a pair of ornamental swords, their metal blades inlaid with silver, which were designed more for show than genuine combat. He warned me that they would come off worse against an average steel blade, but I took them off his hands as I have no other option for now.

I estimated it would take ten hours before we reached our destination on horseback. In the end, it was just over eight.

The journey was uneventful at first. We broke it up by stopping for food and water when we crossed over into Hanover Parish. We found a good inn there, remote and quiet, but I didn't want to stay still for too long, for fear of losing vital time in our quest. It was shortly after this that we had a strange encounter.

By now it was noon, and the sun was at its fiercest. I spied a group of figures on horseback in the distance ahead. The sun was behind them and there was a haze around the group, providing a remarkable silhouette that was entirely unfamiliar. My first thought was I was experiencing some kind of mirage; the figures resembled the legendary Arabians from the pages of *The Arabian Nights' Entertainment*. But as they drew closer, I saw it was a group of blacks. Unlike the slaves I'd encountered all over the West Indies, these looked like royalty.

"Maroons," said Rose.

There were eight of them, all on horseback. At the forefront was the most noble black man I have ever seen. He wore a ruffled shirt with a scarlet cuff under an elegant blue coat. His white linen breeches puffed at the ends and he wore no shoes. A sword swung from his hip and a gun hung from his shoulder. It was obvious he was of high rank. Behind him followed some women and a couple of male attendants, all dressed unusually, but not as flamboyantly as their leader.

I put my hand on my sword. "What are the Maroons?"

"You don't know about Maroons?"

"No. Why are they dressed this way, and who are their masters?"

"The Maroons are free men. They live in the mountains."

This surprised me somewhat. "Have the British not tried to capture them for slaves?"

"Oh they tried," said Rose. "But those people are too strong."

The Maroons were closer now and Rose made the teeth sucking sound that many of the negroes here make.

"What is it?"

"It is Captain Cudjoe," she said, with a mixture of awe and bitterness. She was impressed despite herself.

I looked over again at the majestic leader. We maintained eye contact for a few seconds, before Cudjoe turned his horse around and guided it to step back from the road, his followers falling in behind him. We continued along the road, while the Maroons watched us intently. As I came level with Cudjoe I turned and met his gaze again. I nodded and we passed by unharmed, without a word being exchanged. I had the unfamiliar experience of feeling myself inferior to a black man.

I didn't look back at first, but a few minutes later I turned again to find they were gone. The whole episode felt like a dream. The excessive heat of the day had burnt into my consciousness, so that I had the sensation I was not myself, rather an explorer in the darkest jungles of Africa.

Some hours later we arrived in Savanna la Mar. I wasted little time in finding out more about the man who appeared in Rose's vision. I made enquiries at the market, and this soon yielded results. I discovered that there is indeed a man named Tom Hartnell, a carpenter, who has lived and worked here for some time, supplying timber to the local merchants, as well as finished products for the richer land owners. It didn't take long to discover the whereabouts of his workshop. Now to consider how to approach him. I'd prefer to obtain information from him through stealth rather than aggression. Perhaps I can gain his confidence and learn what I need to know to lead us to the prize.

It has been an exhausting journey, and I am taking some rest at an inn near the centre of town. Whether we will stay here long or leave immediately depends on what we discover after approaching Hartnell. A local merchant has offered to take my letters to the packet boats harbouring at the port here, so I will send them after finishing this.

I will write another letter shortly. You will think it strange I take up my pen so often, but in all honesty, it is helping me to keep sane in this cursed place. The heat is affecting me, and the nature of this backward culture is drawing me into an evil spell. When I write, at least, I feel I'm talking to you, dear Melchior. I'll look out for the next packet boat and send all I have written as soon as possible.

Until then, I remain your loyal servant,

Captain James Maddern

8

18th March 1766, Savanna la Mar, Jamaica

Cyrus awoke not long after the sun rose. His sleep had been hot and fretful, and he couldn't summon his dreams to mind with any faithful recollection. But what he had retained from his rest was a refreshed commitment to the cause of his freedom. All the fears that had been plaguing his thoughts since his time in the prison came rushing back to his consciousness.

Hearing the rumours of the Maroons had given him renewed hope. Previous attempts at starting an uprising, or even planning one, had been dashed with such ferocity that for many slaves the fear of failure was stronger than the desire for freedom. It took an indomitable will to push for liberty while disregarding the horrific fate at the hands of the whites if they were discovered. And somehow, they always were discovered. Often a slave or house servant would hear whisper of a plot and tell all they knew to their masters, with the hope of avoiding punishment, or even gaining a reward.

Nevertheless, with the Maroons on side, Cyrus believed they had a real possibility of overcoming the white men and seizing power for themselves. And there was a source for frustration. It had never felt closer, and yet he could see no clear way to access it. What part could he play, after all? He had no way of getting in touch with the Maroons and no guarantee that they would allow him into their trust in any case.

He stretched his arms either side of him to loosen his limbs, then climbed out of the scattered rags that formed his bedding. Pulling on his dirty workshop linens, he parted the cloth that covered the window to catch the first gleams of light from the emerging sun. He looked out across a still sleeping Savanna la Mar, towards the sea. The stars were fading as the sky grew less grey and more lucent.

If he hadn't approached the window at this precise moment, he would have missed the figure watching him from the yard at the back of the workshop. It was difficult to see, but from his impression he could swear it was a white man who stole back into the shadows. He strained his eyes further and listened intently, but it now appeared there was nothing there. His imagination, no doubt. Why would anyone spend time spying on this house?

Somewhere nearby a dog barked and something clattered to the ground, cracking the silence of the morning. The first amber rays of the sun were creeping into the town. Cyrus considered investigating the disturbance, but dismissed it as the actions of a cat or some recently nocturnal creature.

He pulled the cloth from the window and threw it to the floor, then turned back to look at the workshop. There was nothing he could do right now regarding the Maroons. His best hope was to bide time until he happened on a chance to go with full permission, enabling him to talk to others around town who may know something. Perhaps Plato would have heard more of the matter. He had to be patient or he risked being punished more severely.

His first task was to tidy up before he started work. Hartnell had been in a bad mood with him since he'd fetched him from the prison, and the two had hardly exchanged words in the past few days. It was with some surprise, then, that he heard the master carpenter's whistles before he saw him step into the workshop. And when he did appear, he had a glow of positivity about him.

"Morning," he chirped. "Don't faff about the workshop. I need you to go on an errand."

Cyrus struggled to hide his delight at this opportunity to get out from under Hartnell and potentially follow up on the news of revolt from the night before.

"We need some new blades for our saws," said Hartnell. "I want you to go to the ironmongers in town and place an order. I have the relevant paperwork here." He handed Cyrus an envelope that he hadn't bothered to seal and turned to leave. Cyrus believed he might even get away without a strict deadline, but just then Hartnell turned and said, "Oh, and don't be back late now, will you? No excuses."

Cyrus nodded. Fine. He would make extra haste on the errand to give himself some time to set the ball rolling. If he was lucky, he might be sent out again to pick up the blades themselves. As soon as Hartnell was out of sight, he bolted out of the door and across the town to Savage's Ironmongers. Again he was fortunate. There was nobody being served so he had immediate access to the proprietor. He handed over the note Hartnell had given him.

Edward Savage was in his mid to late fifties, over six foot tall, with a hard, round belly. "You look flustered, Cyrus," he said. "Getting yourself into trouble with the ladies, are you?"

"I wish that were the case," said Cyrus. "I have no time for such things."

"No time? Ha. When you get to my age, you wonder where all that time went. Looking back, I can't understand what could have possibly been a better way to use my time than to get in trouble with the ladies." His grin revealed a set of broken teeth and blackened gums.

"I don't doubt it," Cyrus replied. "How long before you can get these blades ready?"

"In a hurry, eh? Well, let me see." He opened the envelope and scanned the contents of the note. "Why, this is nothing. I can have that ready by tomorrow morning."

"That is good news. I will tell Master Hartnell immediately."

"You won't stay for a drink?"

"He wants me back," said Cyrus. "I will see you in the morning."

"Right you are. And don't forget, find yourself a lady. And if she's a good one, you stick with her."

Cyrus smiled, nodded and left as abruptly as he'd entered. Now he needed to move fast. The Akan in the prison had mentioned Harold, the innkeeper at the Shark's Head. That made sense – Harold heard everything worth hearing in the town. If anyone knew anything, it would be him. Cyrus calculated he had just enough time to slip over there and make some enquiries, before returning to Hartnell within a reasonable time. He felt a surge of excitement at this unforeseen opportunity, and charged towards the Shark's Head.

9

18th March 1766, Savanna la Mar, Jamaica

Cyrus didn't bother to knock on the door of the *Shark's Head*. He pushed against it and it swung open. Standing for a moment in the open doorway, he felt the physical impact of the air escaping from the darkness within, as the smell of stale rum, sweat and tobacco slapped his face on its way past him and out into the street. There was a saltiness in the air, a mix of the sea spray that wafted off the clothes of the sailors who haunted the place, combined with the tanginess of sweat and semen from the cut-throats and whores who used the upper rooms.

Even though it was bright daylight outside, darkness had taken command of the interior. There were windows, but they were almost opaque from years of filth and smoke. None of the lanterns were lit, so it appeared that night lingered forever in this lugubrious room. Cyrus had spent nights there in the past, when a mixture of darkness, lively music, loud talk and free laughter made it exciting, almost glamorous. A visit in the day, though, revealed the true condition of the place.

Cyrus peered through the gloom towards a shadow that shifted in the corner of the bar area. As his eyes adjusted he made out Harold, the old innkeeper, wiping glasses in a slow, mannerly fashion that made it look like an excuse for avoiding something more important that he should be doing elsewhere.

Harold was an eerie sight at the best of times. He was born of two black parents from different parts of the African continent, but he was pale for a negro, and something about the texture of his skin made him glow like a ghost in the shadows. His face was covered with pockmarks and he wore a patch to cover his gashed eye, the worst of many scars he bore from violent encounters.

"Cyrus!" Harold's hoarse rasp sounded like a distant shout but emerged at the volume of a whisper. "What bring you here? It too early for rum today."

Cyrus smiled. Harold was one of the few inhabitants of this town, or anywhere on the island for that matter, who showed camaraderie towards him. It lifted his spirits, though he knew it wasn't personal. He'd seen the same behaviour dished out to one and all who entered the Shark's Head. Harold maintained a jovial disposition at all times, as if nothing bothered him. But Cyrus had heard tales of this man's dark side. You couldn't run a place like this without getting into violent scrapes on occasion, and by all accounts Harold could turn nasty as fast as a falcon on a rope if someone slighted him. Word was that he'd given vicious beatings to those who owed him money, and he'd even murdered someone for crossing him. In a town like Savanna la Mar, you didn't create an enemy out of someone like Harold.

"I'm here for information," said Cyrus.

Harold stopped wiping the glass and regarded Cyrus with his one good eye. "Go on."

"I've heard something," said Cyrus. "About the Maroons."

"What about them?"

"There's ... well, there's talk of a rebellion."

At this Harold's smile slipped from his face. "Why you bothering me about this?" he grunted.

"I heard you might know something."

Harold leant on the bar, bringing his face closer to Cyrus's. "Now listen. I don't know whether you straight up interested, or asking on behalf of your father, but no way I getting dragged into anything that might have me swinging by my neck, seen?"

"I am not working for Joseph Cornishe, I can assure you. My goal is to gain freedom. The freedom that our people deserve."

"Our people?" Harold threw back his head and laughed. "What people are they? Ibo? Creole? Congolese? You ain't none of them, no?"

"I'm on the side of all of them," said Cyrus. "All of those who suffer."

Harold stared at him for a few seconds. "I heard something, it's true. The Maroons, them that live in Accompong, Trelawney, they been getting pissed off."

"Trelawney," said Cyrus. "Cockpit Country. But they have always been supportive of the whites. A few of the slaves at the Black Castle Estate escaped there when I was a boy. The Maroons brought them back and were paid handsomely for it."

"Things have changed, from what I hear," said Harold.

"It must be a pretty big change if they're thinking of taking on the government."

Harold leaned in closer, so that Cyrus could feel the older man's breath on his face. "Some of them whites done them wrong. The Maroons are proud people. Hell, for years the white militia couldn't touch them. The treaty kept peace for long time. But this thing, whatever it was, it made them mad. Madder than ever. The whites best beware, because when Maroons want something, there ain't no one can stop them."

Cyrus felt a surge in his chest. "What if we can help them? With so many slaves on the plantations, all we need to do is co-ordinate our attack and this island could be taken." He paused to let Harold take this in. "Do you know how I could get a message to them?"

Harold laughed again. "Ain't nobody going to be your messenger, boy. You take my advice and stay out of it. The Maroons can look after themselves. Rebellions never end well for slaves though."

Cyrus nodded. "You know, one day soon, we're going to take over this island. And I want to be there when we do."

"Well, you just let me know," smiled Harold. "I'll be right here serving the rum to whoever want it."

Cyrus slipped out onto the street. He almost expected to catch someone watching his movements, but the road was empty both ways. He had to get back to Hartnell's, before his time away raised suspicions. Now all he needed was to find someone who could help him get to Cockpit Country.

🦋 10 🦋

18th March 1766, Savanna la Mar, Jamaica

To Dr Melchior Croll, Bristol, England
    From Captain James Maddern

As promised, I have sent a packet of my previous letters by the ship, Godolphin. My own vessel, the Black Prince, remains moored in the harbour with a few retained crew members, awaiting my return. What I have to tell you today is of the greatest import.

I decided it was time to follow up on Rose's vision and discover what this man Tom Hartnell knew. I enquired around and soon got an address, and Rose and I made our way to Hartnell's property. There was little evidence of activity, so we stole around the back of the property to observe more closely. I was looking for signs of activity when one of the blinds opened and an indistinct face appeared. Whoever it was, he shot a glance towards us, but I moved into the shadows to avoid detection.

As if reading my mind, Rose asked what we were to do at this point, and I considered our options for the first time, for I had devised no plan.

"Let us find somewhere to stay tonight," I said. "I wish to discover as much as possible from this Hartnell fellow. Our appearance at his door should not seem unnatural. We will return when we are at more leisure to compose ourselves."

We went back into the town to secure a base for our stay here. It is thanks to your significant financial support that we were able to find somewhere discreet and decent. I explained to the proprietor that Rose was my maid, and although I received sceptical looks, no further questions were asked. We had one room between us at the inn, and I asked that there be a separate bed made up for Rose. I determined to sleep between her and the door, to prevent her escape. She is technically my property now, but I doubt she has any loyalty to me. In truth she has nowhere to run, but I would rather be sure that she stays with me, at least until the object of our quest is discovered.

The next day we went to Hartnell's house with our plan in place. I was to pose as a recently arrived gentleman looking to set up home in Jamaica, along with my slave Rose. I prepared a credible story: I was visiting because I'd heard that Hartnell made excellent furniture, and I'd like to investigate some purchases for my new home. During this process I hoped to get closer to the man and discover what I could of his personal affairs.

We arrived first thing in the morning, just as the workshop was opening for business. Hartnell himself opened the door, and the first thing I noticed about him was what he wore around his neck: a leather thong with a large, yellowing canine tooth hanging from it. We were getting closer; I didn't need the power of Obeah to sense that.

Hartnell took our story without question, and welcomed us into his house to view some of the items he'd been working on. "I also have an apprentice who works with me, but he's in town on an errand at present," he told us.

Realising this presented an opportunity to discover what he might know about our interests, I engaged in some small talk. "I couldn't help but notice the strange ornament around your neck," I remarked. "Is that from a tiger or lion or some such predator?"

He gave me a lingering look. "Wolf," he said, as he fingered the token. I expected some elaboration, but none came.

"A wolf? It brings to mind the stories I've been hearing about these parts."

"What stories?"

"Oh, the tales concerning the so-called man-beast of Westmoreland Parish. You must be familiar with them."

"Pah," he replied. "Superstitious bollocks. I'd pay no mind to that." The question had irked him. Before he could lead us off the subject, though, I pressed him further.

"I have been travelling through the West Indies, Mr Hartnell, and I can assure you that some of those superstitions are taken very seriously indeed by those who indulge them."

Hartnell's face was like a mask. He seemed to contemplate me more carefully now. "What is it that you're here for, Captain?"

I noticed at this point that he had his hand on one of the carpentry tools on his desk, a hand-held blade.

"I told you, I'm here to buy furniture," I replied, smiling.

"Where exactly is it that you're moving to?"

"I'm looking at a place down by Bluefields Bay."

"There are no properties for sale in Bluefields Bay. I'd know about it if there were."

"It's not something that's on the market as such. Just a conversation ..."

Hartnell looked at me suspiciously, and then turned aside. "I'll show you some of my more expensive stuff, if you like. There's a property near here that's got some of my workmanship on show."

"That would be marvellous."

"Please, wait here a minute, I'll fetch my keys."

He left the room, and I took the opportunity to look around his office. I stole a cursory glance at one of his workshop desks and my eyes alighted on a small bundle of letters, around twenty or so of them, bound together by string. Each one was still in its envelope, with a seal depicting the side-on view of a wolf's head, baring its teeth. I told Rose to keep an eye on the door, and pulled out one of the letters. I scanned it quickly, and this is what I read:

While he is with you, you must keep a careful eye on him. As you know, he is ignorant of his true condition, and we don't know if, or how, it may be realised. He is a demi-sang creature, born from a union of opposites. Whether he will reach an age when his transformation becomes inevitable, or whether it requires some supernatural influence to inspire it, I know not. But until such a time as these questions are answered, he must be kept ignorant of his true nature. Indeed, it may never be a part of his destiny, and that would surely be for the best. He will be visiting Black Castle soon. Please send a note with him, assuring me that you've read and understood this.

I scanned the rest of the letter and learned that it came from a gentleman named Joseph Cornishe. The address was given as Black Castle Estate, Westmoreland Parish.

I wondered, who is this specimen that they were discussing? Presumably a slave, perhaps a result of some diabolical experimentation. And from the content of this letter, this man was on his way back to the Black Castle Estate, or there already. This laid out our subsequent course of action clearly. We must reach Black Castle Estate as soon as possible, to discover what is going on there and what role this Joseph Cornishe has to play in it all.

Rose gave a "yip" from the doorway to indicate that Maddern was returning, so I thrust the letter back into its packet and turned to face the door. Maddern walked in, eyeing me intently.

"Thank you for your time today, Mr Hartnell," I said. I looked up as I uttered these words, only to see Hartnell push Rose aside and lunge towards me, the blade of a sword flashing. I had but a split second to react before I'd have felt that blade through my chest. I parried his thrust with my forearm, and pulled my own knife from my belt as he stumbled past me. His own momentum took him to the floor, where he fell to his hands and knees. The sword slipped from his grasp and I swooped on it. I knelt on his back before he could rise, grabbed his hair and yanked his head upwards, holding the blade to his throat.

"Well, Mr Hartnell, you've somewhat forced my hand. I need to find out more about a certain secret you're keeping. I have no intention of hurting you. Just tell me everything you know and I'll let you go."

"How did you find us?" he gasped.

"That's not your concern. But if you value your life, you'll tell us more about this *demi-sang* that you're harbouring."

I could sense Hartnell tensing his muscles and gritting his teeth.

"I am sworn to secrecy," he said, without a trace of fear in his voice. "This is a power that no man can contain. You would be well advised to turn away now, before you're confronted by something more terrible than your darkest nightmares."

"So be it," I said, more out of bluff than resolve. I had no desire to harm him, but I had to get him to talk. I pressed the blade tighter against his throat.

What happened next occurred so quickly that I was unable to respond. Hartnell yanked his head around, deliberately pushing his throat into the blade. He'd gone for the quickest possible way out, severing his jugular. Rose screamed. I dropped Hartnell's body and watched it go into spasm, sending blood spurting onto the walls. The look on his face as this happened haunts me still. His eyes were wide open, all the time his blood pumping violently out of his freshly cut throat. Rose was wailing, and I shouted at her to calm down. She held her hand to her chest and gulped down her shrieks, staring in horror at the dying Hartnell, whose body jerked as the life spurted out of him. It reminded me of the way I'd seen chickens die on farms in the West Country back in England.

Finally his spasms slowed, and the blood flowed less urgently, until his body lay still. However, his eyes remained wide open and staring right at me, giving me the eerie sensation that he was still watching for what I'd do next. I felt a little faint from the violence of it, but I saw that Rose was breathless with horror and I forced myself to take action. I was in charge of this operation and I needed to keep a strong bearing.

"He can tell us nothing now," I whispered to Rose. "We need to search this house and discover anything he knows about the immortal. We can have no doubt that he's been harbouring what we're looking for."

"What will we do with him?" she replied, a tremor in her voice.

"We'll have to leave him here. If we attempt to hide the body, it will only open us up to more risk. No one knows we're here. As long as we can get out of this without being seen, we'll raise no suspicions."

First I frisked the dead body. He had nothing on him, although my search did reveal a curiosity: a small tattoo on his right wrist depicting the image of a wolf's head. After a hurried look around I found nothing else of significance in Hartnell's office, but I was struck by the number of instances I came across the wolf insignia, which I'd already seen on the seal of the letters. The same symbol appeared as the carved handle on a walking stick, as a figure chiselled into the design on the back seat of his office chair and on an ink stamp that might be used on correspondence or commercial documents.

What was of most interest, however, was a series of sketches on loose leaves of paper. These combined to form a scrapbook containing the weirdest expressions, with detailed drawings of various chimeras, man-beasts and other mythical beings. Although some of these were clearly the work of Hartnell's own hand, others were ripped from books and academic papers. These beasts were represented in a variety of historical contexts, such as medieval European romances, African jungles, the woods of England and the plains of Asia. I had no time to analyse these in any detail at the scene of our crime, so I crammed the whole scrapbook into my shore bag, along with the other letters I'd found, and hurried to get Rose and myself out of there before we were discovered.

We are now back at our temporary residence in Savanna la Mar. We've left behind the corpse of a man whom I had no intention of harming. I believe I acted out of self-defence, but it has shaken me, I won't deny it. I want nothing more now than to leave this town as soon as possible. While we're here there is always the concern that we could be connected to the murder of Tom Hartnell. Besides, we now have tangible written evidence of what we've been looking for. I believe we can source more answers still from this Cornishe fellow. I will make no delay in discovering who he is and where we can find him. Expect more correspondence as soon as I have something further to tell you.

Until then, I remain your loyal servant,

Captain James Maddern

18th March 1766, Savanna la Mar, Jamaica

The talk with Harold had lifted Cyrus's mood. Now he was sure the Maroons were really involved, he began to let himself believe. Here was the opportunity he'd been waiting for. An opportunity to become free, and maybe even lead others to freedom.

The streets of Savanna la Mar were busy now. Shops were opening for the day, slaves were being sent out to collect goods for their masters, and the business of the sugar economy was grinding back into gear. Cyrus loved being part of the town. He'd despised everything about his rural existence growing up on Black Castle Estate, and had made up for his boredom by absorbing all the ideas he could glean from his father's books. The great philosophers and essayists helped form his views on the world, and expanded his mind beyond that country life. It made him want to be part of a larger culture, to contribute to the intellectual theories that were driving European thought forward into a new age. When he was growing up, Savanna la Mar was his nearest big town, but his horizons lay beyond that. Once he became a free man, he could see himself moving to Kingston and starting a university there. He envisioned an enlightened culture in the West Indies: one to rival Paris, London and the other great European capitals. More than anything he wanted to show the white Europeans that there was a future for the children of Africa too.

With all this on his mind, Cyrus rounded the corner at the end of the street where he lived and worked, without noticing much of what was going on around him. It was only when he got to the doorway of Hartnell's workshop that he sensed something was wrong. Normally, the windows and doors to the workshop were open throughout the day, letting in light and air to the dusty working environment. But here he found the door firmly shut. He pushed it open and walked into the room. The blinds were down and the gloom made him blink for a couple of seconds. The first thing he saw was the blood that stained the walls. He looked down to see Hartnell's body, the head contorted at a grotesque angle. He looked like a broken doll. Cyrus dropped to his knees and put his hand in front of the man's mouth. Nothing. He placed his hands hard on his chest. No heartbeat either.

Cyrus sat on the floor and took in deep breaths, gulping back his panic. Questions crowded his brain. Why would someone kill Tom Hartnell? Had they stolen something from him? What would he, Cyrus, do now? Would he be suspected of this murder? These thoughts ricocheted around his head before the emotion arrived in a sudden, shocking surge.

Hartnell was dead.

This man had been more of a father to him than Joseph Cornishe. He was his master, yes, but also his mentor, his teacher, his protector. He'd lived with Hartnell for over six years, since he was fifteen years of age. He was like family. He glanced again at the body and was startled to see Hartnell's eyes wide open and staring directly at him. Was this an involuntary reaction of a corpse? Or was there some life left in him? As if to confirm, Hartnell let out a gurgling gasp and dribbled blood onto the floor beneath his chin.

Cyrus held his head in his hands. "What happened?" was all he could think to say.

"Th ..." gurgled Hartnell, before spewing another mouthful of blood. "The ... they're ... g ... going ... for your ... ff ... ff ... father."

"What?" gasped Cyrus. "Who is going for my father?" He stared into Hartnell's green eyes, which now appeared half opaque, as if they were looking right through Cyrus.

"Only ... you ... Cyrus ..."

"Only me what?"

"Only ... you can ... help him. You must ... go back ... there now. Before ... they get ... to him ..."

With his last words, Hartnell's eyes drifted shut and his jaw slackened. Cyrus held his head for a moment, frozen by the shock of seeing his mentor die. Then he gently laid him to rest on the floor, and looked around the room for more clues as to what might have happened.

There was a lot of blood, but no obvious sign that anything had been taken. Expensive items, such as tools or smaller furnishings, would have been worth reasonable money to anyone with a financial motive, but everything was as it had been when Cyrus had left on his errand that morning.

"Everything all right in there?"

The voice came from outside.

Cyrus jumped to his feet. "Fine. Everything's fine," he shouted back, trying to think fast about what to do.

"That you there, Cyrus?"

He held his breath and composed himself, then hurried towards the door, opened it narrowly and peered outside. It was Jameson, the stonemason who worked nearby.

"Oh, it is you," said Jameson, in his broad Northern English accent. "I saw a couple of people go in earlier."

"Really? There's no one here now."

"That's right, I saw them leave too. Unusual pair."

"These people, what did they look like?" asked Cyrus, as casually as he could muster.

"Oh, very distinctive. A tall white man, with a black girl about your age."

"Probably just a customer and his slave," said Cyrus, desperate to get rid of Jameson.

"Perhaps. I saw them from my window. They stood outside talking for a little while and then went in."

Cyrus shrugged.

"Well, you're back now. Is your master there?"

"What? Oh, yes. I mean, he's not here, but he's fine."

"That's strange. I saw those two leave about half an hour later, but I never saw him go."

"He must have gone out the front. I'm sure he'll be back soon."

"Right you are. Well, tell him to come by when he gets back. I've got a customer wants some furniture fixing. Rich one, too. Probably a good deal of work in that for him."

"I will, yes." Cyrus stood at the door, and for a moment Jameson paused, giving Cyrus a searching look. Then he tipped his head and turned away.

Once he'd gone, Cyrus closed the door and looked back to where the corpse of Hartnell lay. "Goddamn," he uttered, his hands gripping and un-gripping as he scrambled for ideas on what to do next. Why hadn't he told Jameson about Hartnell's dead body, and his dying words? Jameson was one of the few white men he could trust. Now it would be doubly hard to convince anyone that he wasn't a part of this, or at the very least that he was trying to cover it up.

On the one hand, he felt a debt of gratitude for Hartnell and all he'd done for him. It pained him enormously to see him dead. But on the other, Hartnell had been the agent of his tormentor and gaoler, his father Joseph Cornishe.

If these mysterious visitors were on their way to kill Cornishe, Cyrus felt no urge at all to warn him. The real opportunity, now he thought about it, was the realisation of his liberty. If he could make headway before anyone discovered Hartnell's fate, he stood a good chance of making it to the Maroons in Cockpit Country. His future would be determined by whether he grasped this moment or let it go.

One thing Cyrus knew for sure: if he was going to run to the Maroons, he had to act fast. He charged into Hartnell's office and pulled out all the drawers. There was more cash than he expected. He stuffed the money into his pocket without counting. Tickets that gave him permission to travel. He needed these in case anyone stopped him to ask what he was doing. And what was this? A letter with a seal on it, addressed to Joseph Cornishe. The seal bore the design of a wolf's head. Curiosity overwhelmed him. He broke the seal and tipped out the letter inside.

Mr Cornishe,

Your son's behaviour has been alarming me of late. He has always been a strong-willed young man, which is to be expected for one his age. But there's something new in him that's come out in the past few months, a contrary streak that goes far beyond his usual stubbornness. Plato tells me he has started talking about rebellion. I am not convinced he's entirely serious about this – it may well be just a phase in his growing maturity – but I'd rather be cautious and raise the issue now, than be forced to reveal it to you when it's too late and he's already in trouble.

On another matter, I heard a rumour that may be of some importance. As you know, I have people with ears to the ground. They have picked up wind of a traveller from England, recently arrived in Montego Bay from Hispaniola. He's been asking questions, questions of a particular kind, that are pertinent to our interests. I'll alert all our agents in the territory. If they report anything that strikes us close to home, or even a suspicion that someone is on our trail, I'll let you know straight away. I can explain more about this when I see you next.

I await your reply on these matters.

Your faithful servant,

Tom Hartnell

Cyrus put the letter down on the desk in front of him and stared at it. There was so much to surprise him in its contents that he didn't know how to start making sense of it. The tone, for one, was surprising considering the relationship between his father and Mr Hartnell. And what were these interests of which Hartnell spoke?

A bloom of anger spread from his chest outwards like ink on blotting paper. So his father had been spying on him, keeping tabs on his behaviour, through the person of Tom Hartnell. And Hartnell himself, a man he thought he could trust, was reporting on Cyrus's bad behaviour. As for Plato, he'd find a way to get back at that turncoat for what he'd done. He'd confided in that slave because he'd trusted him.

Once again, Cyrus fell in between everyone and everything. Owned and controlled by the whites, distrusted and betrayed by the blacks. It itched inside him to be free of both and to create his own destiny. To be true to himself and not to take the word of trust, nor any preferred support, from these men who were intent on his downfall.

He found a small satchel in the corner of Hartnell's bedroom and filled it with spare clothes, most of the money and the tickets he'd found, and the unsent letter from Hartnell to Cornishe. He crammed the remaining money and his current ticket into his trouser pockets. If the bag was stolen, at least he'd have these essentials. Taking one last look around, Cyrus knew he would not miss this place. The work had stifled him and the position had frustrated him. It was just another cell in the prison of his life.

He turned and barged through the door. Out in the yard he looked up at the sky and breathed in deeply. Here it was, then. He would count this as his first day of freedom. Day one of his new life.

❦　II　❦

✣ 12 ✣

18th March 1766, Queen Square, Bristol, England

Melchior Croll stood at the head of the long oak table, regarding the distinguished men who sat before him. They were thirteen in total. The number was significant, and the men themselves had been chosen carefully. These were amongst the finest minds of their generation: intellectuals, wealthy merchants and deep thinkers. They were all here at the personal request of Melchior Croll himself.

He coughed and addressed the gathering. "You may have some inclination as to why you are here, but not the specifics. I have chosen to share some knowledge I have gained on subjects that are close to our interests, with the hope that we may make progress. As some of you know, I was privileged enough to enjoy private conversations with the antiquarian William Stukeley before he died so tragically last year. He told me some details about the activities of Sir Isaac Newton, details that contradict some of what he published in his biography of that great man. In that book he claimed Newton 'rescued chemistry from the fond inquiry of alchemy and transmutation'. He painted a picture of a man with conformist views who was against esoteric knowledge. But by his own private admission, this is far from the truth. Newton was passionately addicted to the idea of alchemy. He chose never to speak publicly about it. Newton preferred to express his ideas through the lens of empiricism, but he and his followers were formulating their theories around the mythology of the Egyptians, Greeks and pagan priests of Europe. The group, known as the Newtonian Magi, have kept these ideas alive, nurturing them through secret societies and Freemasonry."

A gentleman in the middle of the table interrupted him. "That would explain his survey of Stonehenge and Avebury. He talked much of the Druids."

"Exactly so, Mr Linton," replied Croll. He wiped his brow. He was a heavy man and for him the exertion of standing alone was enough to make him perspire. "Now it so happens that the papers described to me by Stukeley have come into my possession."

A murmur swept across the table.

"Newton's private papers?" exclaimed a gentleman to his right.

"The very same."

"But how?"

"That information I cannot share. The pertinent fact is this: these papers reveal that Newton made some major strides forward. Not in alchemy. In that, he was as frustrated as every other chemist throughout history. No, rather in an area of enquiry that is even more valuable to the betterment of mankind. The nature of immortality itself."

"But we had given up that search," said a stout gentleman

at the front of the group. "No one truly believes in the possibility of achieving immortality any more, do they?"

"We have been roundly censured for even contemplating such a thing," said another of the attendees, a grizzled scarecrow of a man who sat at the far end of the table. "Jonathan Swift publicly mocked the Newtonians for it."

"Gentlemen, I am here to tell you that immortals do exist," Croll announced. "In fact, my own research into the field has rewarded me with some startling insights. I long ago discovered there are certain types of human who have the ability to present themselves in a form that is something other than themselves. Or at least, that ability has been thrust upon them."

"This sounds like fantasy," sneered the scarecrow. "How can you be so sure of the existence of such beings?"

"Because I've met one," said Croll.

Gasps, followed by more muttering.

"An old acquaintance of mine was gifted this condition. Unfortunately, he saw it as a curse, wanted me to help him get rid of it. We worked together on it for a short time, during which I had plenty of opportunities to observe him. In the end he took something precious from me and ran. I'm afraid that specimen has slipped out of my grasp. But recently rumours came back to me that a similar creature has been spotted in the West Indies. And so I have sent a devoted acolyte of mine to see if he can discover it."

"And what has this to do with Newton?" said the stout gentleman.

Croll paused, sensing he had his audience on the hook now. "Newton's papers reveal that he had intimate knowledge of immortal beings such as this. More than that; he had worked out a method of distilling the essence of their immortality, in such a way as it could be shared with others." He paused again to let the enormity of this sink in.

"Are you suggesting," said an elderly gentleman whose sunken features made him look close to death but whose vibrant voice sounded full of life, "that Newton discovered a way to make any man immortal?"

"That is precisely what I am saying," said Melchior Croll. "And soon I shall gain the means to do it. But in order to do so, I will require the assistance of every man in this room."

✻ 13 ✻

18th March 1766, Belmont Estate, Jamaica

Cyrus was dreaming of freedom. He rarely remembered his dreams, but this one was a constant. It was always the same – a dark, starless night; he was in some kind of wood or forest, but it was not in Jamaica. He could sense it was colder, but the cold was somewhere outside him. Within himself he felt a warmth that fully embraced him, like a burning coal that ignited his entire body. He felt heavier, but he wasn't wearing clothes. He was running through the forest. He looked up to see the trees were randomly blotting out the sky above, with dark canopies through which he glimpsed a bright white moon, round and full like a pregnant dove. His body didn't feel like his. It felt more powerful and, in a way he couldn't quite discern, more real.

In his dream he came to a clearing and stopped. He was dreaming lucidly and thought he knew what would come next. It always ended this way. Except this time, it was different.

Instead of a wild animal in the centre of the clearing, bleeding and limping from its wound and primed for his hungry jaws, it was a human body. A slave girl, naked, face down, inert. He stepped forward and reached out to touch her. His intention was to help, but he was horrified to see that his hand had transformed into a fistful of claws, long and deadly like the knives the field slaves used to cut the sugar cane.

The girl in his dream turned to face him just before his claws reached her. She looked confused, unaware of where she was. He couldn't make out her face, but once she had shaken off her sleep, he could sense her horror. He could see the girl's eyes clearly now, and what shocked him was that in those eyes he caught a reflection of himself. And it wasn't his face that he saw, but that of a large snarling wolf.

The girl in his dream screamed and Cyrus lurched awake, on his face and body a sheen of clammy sweat. He looked around him. He was lying on the ground in the midst of a grove of pimento trees, their berries and leaves giving off a sweet, spicy scent. He was well sheltered here, invisible to anyone who didn't come too close to the grove. He wiped his face with his hands and shook his head.

He had been travelling for seven hours now and during that time he'd managed to avoid any confrontations, but his journey had been strenuous. The Maroon settlement in Accompong was on the edge of Cockpit Country. From his starting point in Savanna la Mar, he'd calculated that his best route was down the coast, past Bluefields Bay, then swinging inland to follow the road north. He'd taken a map from Tom Hartnell's belongings, and estimated that he could do the journey in sixteen hours. He'd left Savanna la Mar just before midday, when the heat of the day was at its worst. Consulting the map, he'd estimated that he'd reached the end of the coast path and was approaching Belmont Estate. Taking a break at the edge of the grove, he'd looked out across the hills that dipped down below him onto the shore. He must have fallen asleep, as that was where he'd awoken, moments before.

As he took in the view again, he reflected on how much he loved this island. The air was rich with the scent of the pimento berries, mixed with orange and lemon blossom from the hills. Before him was the translucent green sea, fringed by mangroves and coconut trees. Behind him rose the glossy green hills and mountains, with their rows of broad-leaved banana and plantain trees. He wanted to take it back, rescue it from these people who had invaded from across the water. The whites had all but killed off the natural inhabitants, the Caribs and the Arawaks who were born here, dubbing them savages and cannibals to justify their killing. Now it was a land that was playing host to these white invaders, interlopers that had scarred this country, with no more respect for the island than they had for the slaves who worked it. They fooled themselves with the belief that they 'owned' this land, and fought over it with others from Europe, like children fighting over toys. Cyrus knew that land couldn't be owned, but if anyone had a claim to take over this land it was the black men, not the whites.

The negroes were the ones who worked it, dug its earth, swam its waters and built its homes, farms and fields. The slaves were in touch with the land in ways that Europeans could barely imagine. They could easily take it from the white men and possess it as their own. Once deprived of their guns, the ruling power, such as it was, would fall away, like the skin off a snake. They would be too weak to resist, with no natural resilience to cope in an environment that never welcomed them. They would be set adrift in a land that would happily bury them under its soil.

Besides, none of the white men fitted in here, and they

were acutely aware of it. Cyrus found it hard to rationalise the image of the Europeans that he gleaned from books he read by Fielding, Defoe, Smollet and Voltaire. They painted pictures of an ordered, rational society, one that he could not reconcile with the horrific behaviour of the ruling class in Jamaica. Their behaviour was not only uncivilised, it was savage. Cyrus had seen them treat their slaves worse than animals. Like the driver at Black Castle Estate who had punished one of his field slaves by forcing another slave to shit in his mouth, and then wired it shut for the rest of the afternoon. Or the overseer who had slaves burnt alive when they were caught stealing. You would not read of behaviour like this in these European books. Intellectuals would write of enlightenment, natural philosophy and the elevation of man's culture to the level of the gods, but they paid no heed to the horrors that were being perpetrated in these faraway lands.

Cyrus was distracted from his thoughts by an ominous rumbling sound, like distant thunder. As he turned his attention to this he realised it was drawing closer, and not thunder at all, but something heavy and ineluctable that he could feel through his feet.

"Horses," he whispered to himself.

Whoever it was, he didn't want to risk piquing their curiosity. They might well want to know why a lone non-white was on the move. He couldn't judge how far away the riders were, but he sensed it must be close from how clearly he heard and felt the approaching hooves. He withdrew into the trees and sat listening. Soon he heard neighing a little way down the track, and presently the sound of voices just in front of him. They were passing directly by him, but then stopped on the track, much closer than was comfortable. He peered out of the trees. Three dogs accompanied two horseback riders.

"That was our nigger all right, I'd bet my balls on it," said a voice, close by.

"If he's wanted for murder, he'll be dangerous," said another.

"Yeah. That carpenter in Savanna la Mar was butchered. Only a nigger would do that. And he was the man's apprentice. Learning a trade off him, he was. The ungrateful bastard."

"How does a nigger get to be an apprentice, then?"

"He's a half-caste, ain't he? His old man's the owner of Black Castle Estate. Fucked a black slave girl, and that mongrel is the result."

"He can't have got far. Must be hiding nearby. Let's take a good look around here."

Cyrus sank back into his hiding place. Could he surprise them and take them down? Unlikely. He was carrying a small cutting blade for skinning animals, but there was no way he could stand up to two men with guns. And there were the dogs to avoid too.

"Git boys, go find him," said the first voice, urging the hounds into action. It must have been the direction of the wind, or perhaps the overpowering scents coming across the plains, but the dogs ran off in the opposite direction to where Cyrus was hiding.

Cyrus tried to conceive a plan. If he ran back further into the trees the dogs would hear him and there was no doubt they could catch him easily. But staying put was risky too, as they'd surely pick up his scent at some point. The horses shuffled for a minute, then trotted off in the same direction as the dogs. Cyrus got to his feet and listened carefully. He could hear them in the distance now, moving forward in the direction he was headed. Best for him to wait a while longer before continuing on his journey, or he'd risk catching up with them. He sat down, his back against the tree, and closed his eyes, controlling his breathing as best he could. So someone had discovered Hartnell and alerted the authorities. Of course, he was the prime suspect. He'd known that would be the case, but he hadn't expected so swift a reaction.

Now he had a more urgent plan. Get to the Maroons before the bounty hunters caught him. He'd rest here awhile until he was sure they'd put some distance between them.

❧ 14 ❧

18th March 1766, St Elizabeth Parish, Jamaica

Cyrus shivered as the cold air settled on his tired arms. The gibbous moon hung in the sky like a lantern, and it was bright tonight, bright enough to light the ground in front of him as he walked. Not that there was anything to see in this featureless landscape. Scrubby grassland all around with small plots of trees occasionally cropping up on either side. Monotony didn't begin to describe it. He realised already that he was missing the town, that hotbed of activity and thought. When this mission was over – not just the mission to the Maroons, but the whole mission, the big mission – he would go and live in the biggest city he could find and spend the rest of his days amongst people. Historians, philosophers, artists, authors. People who made a difference to the world.

It had been a few hours since he'd encountered the bounty hunters, and he'd seen no sign of them or anyone else since.

He'd now crossed into St Elizabeth Parish, and was approaching the small settlement of White Hall. Judging by the bad state of the road he was on, it was rarely used.

He stopped to look at his map. He'd been travelling for nine hours or so and he was covering the territory adequately. He estimated it would take another nine or ten hours to reach Accompong. He couldn't afford a full night's sleep tonight – it would slow him down too much. He calculated that if he restricted himself to three hours' sleep during the dark hours, he could be there by nine or ten o'clock the next morning.

All of this was going through his mind when he felt himself pulled backwards onto the side of the path. The sting of a cold blade bit into the skin of his neck.

"Don't move a muscle, nigger."

Cyrus gulped and the blade cut into him deeper. "I have a ticket."

"Fuck your ticket. We know who you are. And we've been told to take you back alive, so it's better for both of us if you stay still."

Cyrus's brow pulsed. He could probably overpower the man holding him, but he doubted he'd be able to evade the other man as well. And there were the dogs, who could bring him down if he chose to run. Stalling was his only option.

"I'll come quietly."

As he relaxed, his aggressor pulled both Cyrus's arms behind him and tied his wrists together with a strong leather cord, then turned him round to face him. He was a tall, spindly man with a sprout of straggly red hair and a painfully thin face that made him look as if his cheekbones had collapsed. He sneered at Cyrus and then called to his accomplice. Less than a minute later, the other bounty hunter arrived on the scene, with all three dogs in tow.

"You got him," said the man on horseback, a dirty-faced man with stubbly black hair and a stocky frame. He grinned and got down from his horse to take a closer look. "So this is the murdering bastard, is it?" He strode up to Cyrus and grabbed his throat, pushing his face upwards.

"I'm not a murderer!" said Cyrus.

"Of course not. That carpenter cut his own throat, didn't he?"

"I don't know who did it, but it wasn't me."

"Fuck you. If it was up to me, I'd beat you to death here and now."

"I'd like to do the same, Sam," said the other. "But it seems his father wants his boy back home with him."

"My father?" Cyrus whispered.

The first captor looked at him wearily. "Yeah, your father. God knows why he didn't kill you at birth, a man like that. But maybe this little escapade will be enough to convince him for good that nigger blood poisons white man's blood."

Cyrus was reeling. How had there been time for Joseph Cornishe to find out about Hartnell's death and commission a manhunt? His father was forever two steps ahead of him, as if he constantly knew what he would do next. And now here he was, not more than twelve hours into his escape, and he'd been captured by his own father.

"We've heard you're quite the devious one," said Sam. He shoved Cyrus onto the ground so that he landed hard on his back and then spun him over and tied his arms more securely, before wrapping a gag around his mouth. "Get him onto my horse."

They lifted him on and then Sam mounted and sat behind him, taking the reins by wrapping his arms around Cyrus's body. They set off back in the direction that he'd come from.

Cyrus considered his options. Even if he could manage to overpower Sam, he'd still have to dismount and somehow run for freedom with his hands bound behind him, while pursued by a man on horseback and three dogs. For now, at least, he was going to have to let things take him where they would.

❧ 15 ❧

19th March 1766, Black Castle Estate, Westmoreland Parish, Jamaica

To Dr Melchior Croll, Bristol, England
    From Captain James Maddern

Rose awoke screaming last night. She'd had another vision, and this time it wasn't prompted by the ingestion of herbs from an Obeah ceremony. She described seeing through the eyes of a creature and catching the reflection of the creature in the eyes of its victim.

"A werewolf?" I asked.

"I think so," she said. "But different from my other vision."

"Was it in the same place as the first?"

"No, somewhere else. Woods." She paused. "The girl it stalked. It was me." She looked shaken.

"A bad dream, I'm sure," I said.

"Perhaps. It felt more than that. A connection."

We were forced to put this aside, as we had little time to prepare for our journey. Neither Rose nor I had much to pack or carry. I spent some hours making enquiries in the town and discovered the whereabouts of the Black Castle Estate. While there I heard people gossiping about the murder of Tom Hartnell. It seems his apprentice was the main suspect, as the boy has run away. This kept any suspicion away from me, although I needn't have worried on that score. People come and go here with swift regularity, and there is nothing about my person that suggests I have any reason to commit murder.

We rode first to the rural part of Westmoreland Parish. We encountered a crocodile on our way past the swampy wetlands outside Savanna la Mar, which gave me some cause for alarm. We stopped to observe it for a few minutes, but I was careful to keep my distance. Rose knows their ways and informs me they can run alarmingly fast when giving chase and are too strong to fight off if they do catch up with you. She says she once saw a fully grown cow drinking at the river's edge that was pulled in and devoured by a crocodile lying in wait just below the surface. They are fearsome creatures indeed.

We reached the house itself after many hours of travelling, and what a sight it was. The Black Castle is an apt name. It is constructed entirely of dark wood that saps all light, even in the bright sunshine, like a hole in the daylight. As we rode up the long drive I felt some trepidation, and I sensed Rose was unnerved by the place.

I had crafted a simple story to tell when we got there, and I was fully prepared to tell it when the overseer's right-hand man, a white servant called Filton, came out to meet us. I addressed him courteously. "My name is Captain Maddern. I was just passing through this neighbourhood on the way to Kingston, and wondered if I might take a short rest here. I've been riding for days, and confess I am exhausted."

Filton looked wary. "It is not my decision to make," he said gruffly. "Come this way."

I followed him into the house, indicating for Rose to remain outside. Filton asked me to wait in the entrance hall while he went upstairs to alert his master. The Black Castle is a typical plantation house in terms of size and structure, but it felt darker and somehow more ancient than any of the big houses in the West Indies that I've visited so far. The doors to adjoining rooms from the hallway were all closed, leaving the entrance hall devoid of natural light and shrouded in an oppressive gloom. There was a faint odour too, a kind of earthy dampness that felt reminiscent of another time and place, but I couldn't say where or when. On the walls around the hall were highly stylised paintings in an illustrative mode. I leant in to look at the one nearest to me and recognised the subject as Artemis, the Greek deity. She was pictured as a young girl, dressed in a short skirt and hunting boots. She held her bow aloft, her shooting arm pulled back in readiness to loose her arrow into the sky. From her head sprouted proud antlers, but her face showed a delicate grace, a strong and palpable beauty. It was a captivating image painted in such vivid colours that it seemed to float up from its canvas and hang there in the gloom.

My reverie was broken by the sound of footsteps on the stairs. I looked up to see a tall, imposing figure descending towards me. Cornishe looked immaculate in a light blue coat and creaseless cotton shirt. His black boots shone and his wig was perfectly dressed and scented with what smelt like rosemary and lavender.

"Joseph Cornishe at your service, sir," said the overseer, offering his hand.

I was immediately impressed by the presence of the man. It was rare enough to see someone of his height, over six feet tall I'd gauge. But there was something else about his presence that gave the impression of solidity and strength.

"My man explained your predicament," said Cornishe, smiling broadly. "You're most welcome to stay. We have a spare room for you, and your girl can stay in one of the slave huts."

"That is most generous of you, sir," I replied. "I will just need a night's rest and I'll be gone."

"Not at all, it will be my pleasure. I hope you'll join us for dinner. My cook is preparing clucking hen broth and yams, and we have a good stock of wine if you're not averse."

"That would be marvellous, thank you kindly."

"Filton will take your horses to the stables and your slave to her quarters. Please follow me and I'll show you to your room personally."

I drew Rose aside. "Keep an eye out for the creature," I whispered. "Its aversion to silver will betray it. Take this coin and use it if you need to."

Filton reached out to take the reins of the horses and, as he did so, I noticed an identical tattoo to the one I'd seen on Hartnell's wrist, depicting a wolf's head, side on. I gazed a little too long at it, and he must have caught me, because he moved his arm down swiftly as if to hide it from curious eyes. I nodded thanks to him and followed Cornishe into the house.

The wood creaked as we mounted the steps up to the main door and entered into the spacious hall, our footsteps echoing around us. There was a staircase opposite the main door, at the top of which was a large portrait of an austere man in formal wear; obviously an important man. "Who is this?" I asked, pointing to the painting.

"That's Mr Killerton, the owner of the Black Castle Estate. He lives in London. He is an old man now and hasn't visited here for some time."

"He must place great trust in you."

Cornishe smiled. "I've been overseer for over twenty years and I am proud to say I have given no grounds for complaint. Come, I'll show you to your room."

He led me into a generous-sized bed chamber with a large four-poster bed, and a window that overlooked the stables. The room was filled with sunlight, but straight away I felt that heaviness again. I am writing at my desk in here now, and I can't shake the awful feeling it gives me. I feel sealed off from the outside world, as if this room has its own rarefied atmosphere.

I joined my host for dinner an hour or so after he'd left me to get settled in my room. The meal was not an elaborate affair, but simple and tasteful, made up of local ingredients. The house servants served just the two of us and Cornishe asked a few questions, more out of politeness than real curiosity. In truth, throughout the meal he seemed somewhat distracted, one might even say agitated. It came to a point where he merely stared into his meal and probed it with his cutlery.

"Is everything all right?" I asked, to ease the awkward silence more than anything.

"Why yes," he said, making an overt effort to pull himself together. "I was just reminded of something, quite randomly, something urgent that requires my attention. Will you excuse me?"

"Of course," I replied. He stood up, mumbled a goodnight and then strode out of the room. I was quite nonplussed by this and it left me wondering whether it was something I had said, or whether he was really in earnest regarding his forgotten responsibilities.

I saw no more of Cornishe that evening. A few moments after he'd left, Filton arrived to say that his master was deeply engrossed in some urgent business and that he would not be joining me again this evening. Filton offered to show me to my room, but I assured him I could make my own way, and I returned to my foreboding chamber. I write this now by candlelight, with the feeling that we have found our way to something vitally important for our quest, but I am not sure why or how this is the case.

I will not post this for a few days, and of course I have no hope of an imminent reply from you in any case, but I will attempt to learn more from Mr Cornishe when next I see him. For now I will sign off for the evening, and attempt to sleep in this disturbing place.

Until I write again, I remain your loyal servant,

Captain James Maddern

❧ 16 ❧

19th March 1766, Black Castle Estate, Westmoreland Parish, Jamaica

Cyrus groaned. He was lying on his side in a dirty cart whose previous contents were chickens and livestock, judging by the traces of feathers and excrement scattered around. The spindly hunter was driving the horse that pulled this cart, while his accomplice, the stocky man called Sam, was riding alongside on another horse. They'd done nothing to shelter Cyrus from the morning sun, and his face and arms were burning from the heat. It had only been a day since he'd made his bid for freedom but it felt much longer. He wanted nothing more than a soft bed of hay in the shade and a drink of cold water.

It took a few moments for him to realise that the cart had stopped moving. And then the sound of a voice that cut through his agony and struck him like a stiletto to the heart. Joseph Cornishe. His father.

"Get him out of there."

"Will do," said Sam.

The next thing he knew, Cyrus was being pulled out of the cart. His hands were still secured behind his back, and his knees felt weak from sleep, but he determined to pull himself up to full height. As his eyes struggled into focus he saw the familiar figure of his father approaching. At six foot two inches, his was an imposing presence. His face was hardy, tough, like smooth leather, and his features remained as proud and handsome as they'd always been. It was hard to judge how old he was. Joseph would always avoid the question. He had the look of a forty-year-old man, but he never seemed to age, not in all the time that Cyrus had known him.

Cornishe lashed out with his right arm and struck Cyrus across the face. Cyrus's head was knocked backwards by the blow and it took all his strength to stay on his feet. He fought back tears and returned his father's gaze once again. Now he noticed the twitching in his father's cheek, the one tick that he'd learned to look out for as a young boy, a sure sign that his father's bad mood had flipped over into something he couldn't control.

"Filton!" said Cornishe.

Although a little more gaunt of face, the greasy-haired Filton was as obsequious as Cyrus remembered him. "Yes sir."

"Take him to my study."

Filton nodded and took Cyrus by the arm. Cyrus heard Cornishe settling accounts with the bounty hunters behind him as he was led into the house. Once he'd been hauled up the steps, Filton marched him along the main corridor of the Black Castle Estate. The place had retained its magnificence, with its chandeliers, elegant furniture, ornate mirrors and vivid decor. Oh yes, his father liked to show off his wealth all right. And Cyrus saw that his attention to detail, for precise order and meticulous cleanliness, was undiminished.

At the end of the long corridor, Filton shoved him into his

father's study. "Got you by the balls this time, hasn't he, boy?" he said. "Don't think you'll be getting out of this one in a hurry." He bore the same sneer that Cyrus had seen so many times as a child growing up, the sneer that betrayed his utter abhorrence for Cyrus and all he represented.

They stood together in the study, awaiting Cornishe's arrival, and Cyrus took a moment to look around. After a few minutes he heard heavy footsteps, and Cornishe strode past the two of them to his desk, turning to face Cyrus. The struggle to contain his emotions didn't last long.

"How dare you!"

"I didn't kill Hartnell, of course I didn't," said Cyrus.

"Quiet! So. Where the hell were you running to this time?"

"I ... I was going to return," Cyrus heard himself say.

"You insolent wretch. You well know the fate of non-whites on this island. You could have been bound into slavery from the moment you were born. I saved you from that. I gave you a life worth living."

"Saved me?" said Cyrus. "You think I've ever considered myself saved? I've lived in other people's shadows, your shadow, my entire life."

Cornishe reached behind his desk and brought forth a cane. The handle was of a wolf's head in bronze, the same cane that Cyrus had felt batter him whenever he'd made a serious transgression as a boy.

"What am I to do now?" barked Cornishe. "Only yesterday the overseer of the Egypt Estate was lecturing me on how I'm too lenient with my slaves. Your attempt at escape has made me look a complete fool. Your actions have decided this, not mine."

He pointed at him with the cane now, the colour burning his face. Even Cyrus, who made a point of showing no fear, couldn't hide his anxiety. His father was not only taller than him but far stronger. Cyrus remained silent and stared at the floor. He didn't want to submit, but he couldn't look his father in the eyes.

"Where did you think you'd go?" asked Cornishe again.

"I cannot say."

"Cannot? Will not? This better not have anything to do with this bloody plot I'm hearing rumours of."

Cyrus raised an eyebrow.

"Oh yes," continued Cornishe, "don't think I haven't heard talk. They say the Maroons are involved this time. Tell me that you wouldn't be so stupid—"

"I seek only my own freedom," said Cyrus.

"But you *have* your freedom! I've given you much more than any son of a slave would expect in this world." Cornishe's knuckles turned white around the cane and for a moment Cyrus imagined him leaping over the desk and pounding him to a pulp. But then he closed his eyes and took a few deep breaths, pausing for a moment before continuing. "I've been thinking about this since the moment I heard about your escape. I mean to find out about the murder. I know it's not you. On that point, at least, I trust you. But as for running away, that is inexcusable. I've made my decision. You will spend three days in the bilboes."

Cyrus had expected something severe, but not this. However badly he'd behaved in the past, he'd never received any punishment so cruel. And he'd never have expected this of his father. He swallowed his fear and looked up at him with defiance. "Your eagerness to humiliate me explains everything that you need to know about my behaviour."

Cornishe's shoulders heaved. He stared past Cyrus, over his shoulder, to his servant standing by the door. "Filton."

"Yes sir."

"Put him in the bilboes and lock him in the barn."

A sly smile flittered across Filton's face. "Right you are, sir." He turned towards Cyrus and took his arm to lead him out.

"I know the way." Cyrus snatched his arm away and strode straight past Filton. Just as he reached the door, he turned back to Cornishe. "If I'm not a slave, then what am I?"

This question seemed to catch Cornishe by surprise. He gritted his teeth but kept his mouth firmly shut. Cyrus didn't wait to hear any more. He turned and marched from the room, with Filton scurrying after him.

17

20th March 1766, Black Castle Estate, Westmoreland Parish, Jamaica

To Dr Melchior Croll, Bristol, England
    From Captain James Maddern

I woke to the sound of rain hammering the windows of my room. The storm had come out of nowhere and it was fierce. It was a welcome respite from the heat though, which has been stifling these past few days.

I sat up in the dark and rubbed my eyes. The moon was bright despite the rain and it shone into my room like a lamp. In my half-dream state I looked down onto the bed and saw that my bed sheet was no longer covering my legs, but had twisted around them, giving the impression that my limbs had become distorted and misshapen. I dimly recalled a disturbing dream which had seen my darling Claire returned to me, but as a decomposing corpse. It must be a result of the stress. You know that my nerves are shredded by this quest. I have put all my faith in you and can only hope that the pressure I'm experiencing will be repaid with the successful realisation of my dreams.

I was still in a confused state when I heard the sound from beyond my window. The sound of the wind and rain was filling my ears, but there was something else, something distant and remote that seemed to be coming from inside the storm. It sounded like a bestial howl, coinciding with the sound of a door slamming. I got up from the bed and walked to the window, looking down onto the grounds of the Black Castle Estate. It was then I noticed candlelight in one of the rooms on the lower floor and across the courtyard. I could see a tall figure pacing back and forth in an agitated manner, circling the room. His movement reminded me of a hyena that I'd once seen trapped in a cage in an African village.

I looked up to the moon. Waxing gibbous, over two thirds full. A few more days, and if what I'd discovered was correct, someone on this plantation would reveal their secret. I knew I wasn't going to get back to sleep in this storm, and I was curious to know who was awake at this late hour. I wrapped myself in a gown and opened the door, thinking I would make my way to the kitchen to get myself a drink, as this would provide the perfect excuse for my night-time wanderings. I crossed the landing and descended the stairs. The great hallway I'd entered yesterday was much more mysterious in the darkness. The faces of the statues and paintings watched me as I walked amongst them.

At the bottom of the stairs I looked down the long corridor towards the kitchen. This was where I'd seen the figure from my window. There was a row of doors on both sides and no way of knowing which I'd been looking into from the window of my room. I moved down the corridor as quietly as I could, looking up at more paintings as I passed them. Again I noticed a theme to the art. The first painting depicted a great heavenly battle between the demons of Satan and the angels of God. The next showed Satan being evicted from heaven. Each piece of art bore a poetic inscription that I recognised from Milton's *Paradise Lost*.

Stepping forward, I inspected a striking portrait depicting the angel Raphael descending to Earth to speak to Adam, alongside the following lines:

> To all the fowls he seems
> A phœnix, gazed by all, as that sole bird
> When, to enshrine his reliques in the Sun's
> Bright temple, to Egyptian Thebes he flies.
> At once on th' eastern cliff of Paradise
> He lights, and to his proper shape returns,
> A Seraph winged.

As I was reading this, a door at the far end of the corridor opened and someone stepped out. The illumination from the room cast the figure in a half-light but it didn't take me long to recognise Joseph Cornishe. There was a look of anguish upon his face.

"Can I help you?" he said, his speech slightly slurred.

As I drew closer, I could see that his eyes were half-closed. He seemed drunk or medicated in some way.

"I do apologise," I said. "I couldn't sleep. The storm."

Cornishe smiled at this, and some of the anguish appeared to dissipate. "I've been having the same problem. The weather out here can be dramatic, to say the least. Was there anything in particular you wanted?"

"Oh, just a drink of water, that's all. I forgot to take one with me when I retired."

"Why not join me for a glass of wine?" Cornishe said, indicating his study.

"Well, why not indeed?" I followed him into the room. Two bottles stood on the table there, one empty, the other half full. Next to them was a large open book, containing detailed diagrams and tables of planetary motions. "You study the heavens?"

"Yes. Just a hobby." He cast a blurry glance at me. "Did you know that it's the eleventh moon day tonight? The most powerful lunar day of the month. It's no wonder there is such a storm. According to Hindu legends, this day coincides with the awakening of the mystical energy of Kundalini, one of the most powerful forces in the universe."

I looked at him to see if he was joking. Surely a Christian man wouldn't believe such nonsense? The wine talking, perhaps. I began to feel awkward.

"You have been to India?" I asked, to break the silence.

"Sadly not. I spent a lot of time in Europe, but ..." he trailed off, as if realising he'd been drawn into a conversation he didn't want to have. He went over to a cabinet against the wall and pulled down a glass. "How about you, Captain? Have you travelled widely?"

"Europe, Africa, the West Indies – those have been my travelling grounds. I often wished I'd found the time to get to Asia."

"There is plenty of time for you," said Cornishe, pouring a glass of wine and handing it to me.

I smiled. "I don't think I'll have the energy. After this

particular journey I fully expect to return to England and remain there for the rest of my life."

"Once a man has the taste for exploring, it's difficult to get it out of his system," replied Cornishe as he sat down and indicated that I take a seat opposite him.

"Not me. I think I've had my fill of adventures."

"And what adventure are you on right now?"

For the first time I noticed a probing edge to the overseer's voice. It caught me unawares, and I hesitated before replying. "Trade. I've a shipment coming in soon. Some textiles, cloth, that sort of thing. I hope to fetch a good price for them on this island."

Cornishe smiled. "I wouldn't call that an adventure. There is much more to experience on this island than trade."

"Well, I suppose the adventurous part involves some field work while I'm here. Taking samples of the landscape, flora and fauna."

"Interesting. Is this on your own behalf or for an organisation?"

"It is actually to provide an insight into the West Indian environment for my benefactor. He is an intellectual of the highest standing, one of the most knowledgeable men in the whole of England with regards to natural philosophy."

"Really?" said Cornishe. "What's his name? It may be I have heard of him. I have strong interests in these areas myself."

"Alas, his reputation has not extended throughout England, let alone abroad. He likes to be discreet, you understand, unlike those fame seekers more concerned with prizes and connections than the advancement of knowledge. But I am sure in the future, when his most important work is done, many throughout the world will learn of the vital contribution to human knowledge made by Dr Melchior Croll."

I hadn't been looking at his face when I mentioned your name, but I soon became aware that he had fallen silent. I looked up to observe that the colour had entirely drained from his face. It occurred to me now that he wasn't as drunk as I'd first assumed. The wind whistled outside, and rain lashed the window. Once again, I thought I heard a rumbling sound from somewhere outside the house. The wine was strong and even though I'd only taken a couple of sips, it was already affecting me, making my head thick and sluggish.

There was a flash of lightning, the first of the evening, and as I glanced out of the window, my heart leapt at what looked like a human figure crouched on the ground about twenty feet away from us. It brought to mind the figure of a witch, sitting cross-legged on the ground with head bent forward, long locks of hair hanging in front of its face. I barely had a chance to see it before the lightning flash subsided and it was swallowed back into the darkness. I must have physically started, as Cornishe noticed my alarm.

"Did you see something?" he asked, turning to look at the window.

"I ... a form, a woman, I think ..."

Cornishe moved over to the window and peered out. "I'm sure no one would choose to be out there in this weather. A trick of the light, I'll warrant."

He turned back to face me at the exact moment the lightning lit up the window behind him once again. This time I was able to see more clearly that there was indeed a figure sitting on the ground outside, and that it was Rose. I didn't want the overseer to see what I was seeing, and wrenched my attention back to him.

"Yes, you're right, of course. I'm sorry, I'm feeling somewhat jumpy."

Cornishe smiled again and picked up the bottle of wine,

tilting the neck of the bottle towards my glass. I shook my head and stood up. A bead of sweat ran down my forehead.

"You know, I think I could do with that glass of water."

Cornishe hesitated, the bottle still proffered towards me, and then nodded. "Of course. Allow me to fetch it for you."

As soon as I was sure my host had gone, I rushed to the window and peered out. It was certainly Rose that I saw sat outside. There was a French window in the middle of the wall and I tested its handle. It opened and I slipped outside to speak to her.

"What are you doing out here?" I hissed.

She looked vacant, her eyes wide and empty. "I have found the creature."

"What? Where?" I looked around.

"In there." She lifted her hand and pointed gravely to the room that I had just left.

"You're not suggesting ..."

Cornishe? It did seem as if he'd been hiding something. But that he might be the beast seemed impossible.

"Take this." Rose held out her fist and opened it to reveal the silver coin I'd given her earlier. It glinted in the moonlight under the lashing rain. "Test him. If he avoids silver, you have your proof."

I took the coin. "Wait out here. I may have need of your powers."

I closed the French door behind me, just in time to see Cornishe return, a pitcher of water and a tall glass in his hands.

"It's probably a good thing that the weather's broken," he said. "The humidity was getting unbearable." He bent down to place the pitcher and glass on the table and looked up at me. Then he did something curious. He lifted his head slightly and flared his nostrils, almost as if he was sniffing the air.

I smiled and stepped towards the water. As I did so, I sent

the silver coin clattering to the floor between us. Cornishe stepped back as soon as he saw what it was, and kept his eye fixed on it, as if it were a poisonous reptile. I bent forward and picked it up, but continued to hold it in my hands so that Cornishe could see it.

"I'm grateful to you for letting me stay here, Mr Cornishe. I'd like to give you something to thank you. This coin is rare and very valuable. It's made from the silver mines in the mountains of Cerro Rico in Potosí. If you look here, you can see the mark." I held it up but Cornishe didn't come any closer.

I tossed the coin at Cornishe. It spun through the air in a slow arc that left a trail of silver light behind it. Quicker than the lightning of the storm, the overseer slipped out of the way of the coin, then leapt towards me. The next thing I knew, Cornishe had grabbed me by the throat and was lifting me a few feet off the floor. I looked down in horror at the twisted face of a maniac.

"How did Croll know I was here?" he growled.

I struggled to articulate something but the hand around my neck was so tight that I couldn't speak. The man possessed incredible strength. As my breath shortened, my eyes started to flicker and I felt I was doomed to die here, at the hands of the very one I was seeking. I'd sworn to myself that I wouldn't let that happen. It was my mission, my reason for being here. My dream of a new life back in England, with everything you have promised me. But just as my consciousness began to slip away, something happened. The grip around my neck loosened, and I dropped to the floor. I fell into a heap, and gasped for breath.

When I looked up I beheld an extraordinary scene. Cornishe was backing away, his lips curled into a vicious grimace, like a dog facing up to an aggressor. Opposite him stood Rose, who had entered through the French windows and was holding her arms up in front of her, her head down and eyes closed. She was muttering a mysterious incantation. As her voice rose in volume, I heard her utter the following words in an otherworldly tone – "By the spirit of Eshu!" – at which she flung her head up and her hands outward, pointing them directly at Cornishe.

The overseer stumbled backwards and fell against the door. It was as if she'd thrown a heavy physical object at him. With a pained snarl he fell out into the hall, then leapt to his feet, but rather than return to fight, he ran, his heavy footsteps thudding away into the deeper mysteries of the house.

I rubbed my neck and tried to regain my composure.

"We surprised him," said Rose. "But he will come back at us even stronger."

"Then we must take the fight to him."

(To be continued)

✣ 18 ✣

20th March 1766, Queen Square, Bristol, England

Melchior Croll opened the door to his laboratory and took in a lungful of its stale air. Odours of sulphur, copper and ash filled his chest, and he basked for a moment in the atmosphere of his beloved sanctuary. This was his world.

After locking the door behind him, he hung the keys on the large hook by the side of the frame, took off his coat and draped it on the coat rack. He took another more practical coat, one that was designed to keep his formal clothes clean, and sat at the great bench that dominated the room. On the surface were various scientific instruments: test tubes, flasks, glass jars. As with everything in Croll's life, the whole place was ordered and clean. At the edge of the desk sat a neat pile of papers and books. He picked up one of the books, a slim volume with a plain leather cover and no writing on it. He leafed through it until he found the part he was looking for. There, in black ink against the yellowed pages, was the image of a wolf, its head turned to the side, fangs and teeth flashing, eyes bright and penetrating. Its ears were pricked upwards, its left leg curled beside it, the clawed paw hanging relaxed at its side with its long talons extended. Along its back the fur bristled erect as if it had just been disturbed and was ready to attack.

Croll loved to look at this image. It stirred something within him, something atavistic and primal. He'd given Maddern clear instructions regarding his quest. But he wondered now if it was not just immortality that lured him, but something else, something about the nature of the thing that he coveted. It appealed to something deep within him, a yearning for power. He had often told himself that he would mount the dead creature's hide on his wall as a trophy, or perhaps have it fashioned into a magnificent coat. But recently he saw himself not just wearing the creature's hide, but becoming it. He envisioned himself transforming into the beast, surrounded by acolytes and worshippers, all bowed down to him, allowing themselves to be sacrificed to his eternal hunger. He felt a delicious thrill at the thought of the fear he could instil in others, the boundless power of his existence. With a crack, he snapped the book shut. His patience had been stretched by the wait.

"Lil!" he barked.

"Sir?" The rough female voice came from the store cupboard.

"I need something from you."

A pause. "But I've already given you so much."

"Aye, that you have, my dear. But I need more."

"Is it time, then?"

"Not time now, no, not time now. But it's near. I sense it's near."

Lil parted the curtain that hung over the doorway and

stood leaning on her crutches. She was in her early twenties and slim, with ghostly pale skin and hair dark as midnight. Her left leg was severed at the knee, and scars on her face paid testament to other pains. A dirty bandage covered the place where her left ear had been.

"What will you take from me this time?"

Croll turned on his stool and faced her. "Show me your hands."

With her armpits leaning on the crutches, she held up both arms for his inspection. On her right hand she had her thumb, index finger and little finger. The middle two fingers were missing, livid red scars paying testament to her loss.

Croll grabbed the wrist of her left hand. It was fully intact.

"Balance," he said.

He drew her hand towards his face, pulled at the middle finger and placed it in his mouth.

Lil smiled. "Will it help us get what we want?"

"Oh yes." Now Croll was sucking on her finger, sliding his tongue down its length, letting out a languid groan as he did so. "Just trust me now. Balance will be restored."

❧ 19 ❧

20th March 1766, Black Castle Estate, Westmoreland Parish, Jamaica

To Dr Melchior Croll, Bristol, England
    From Captain James Maddern

(Continued)

I jumped to my feet and ran to the corridor. There was no sign of Cornishe, and the house itself was eerily quiet. I beckoned Rose.

"I'll need the silver blades. Follow me."

We rushed up to my room. I made Rose wait outside while I grabbed one of the swords from my belongings. Out in the corridor Rose had her back to the wall, preparing herself for another attack.

"Perhaps he's gone to get help," I said.

She lowered her head and closed her eyes. I think she was trying to enter the state where she could probe his mind again. But as she was doing so, I heard a voice down the corridor.

"Are you all right, sir?"

It was Filton, Cornishe's servant. I stepped forward to block his path, holding the blade behind my back with one hand and proffering the silver coin with the other.

"I think your master may be in distress," I said. "He ran from me after I'd offered him this silver coin."

He looked at the coin and back at me. "Ah, I see," he said. "It's true he's not been well of late. If I were you, I'd leave him be. I'm sure he'll have recovered by the morning."

"I'm afraid I can't do that," I said.

Before he had time to realise my intentions, I'd pinned him to the wall with my forearm and thrust the blade to his throat.

"I need to know where he is. And if you don't help me, we'll have no further need for you, understand?"

His eyes widened in panic.

"I know what he is," I said. "A werewolf. He ran from us when we discovered him. Where might he have gone?"

He looked at me doubtfully. "What do you want with him?"

"I don't wish him any harm. My benefactor wants him back in England, very much alive and in one piece. Cornishe will help him with his studies."

"You can't subdue him," said Filton. "He's not transformed. That won't happen for a couple of nights yet. But even in human form he has the strength of many men. And he grows stronger nearer his time. Weapons are useless against him."

"Even if they're made with silver?"

Filton looked at the blade. "I see. Silver is poisonous to him, yes."

"Will it kill him?"

"No. Not unless you cut off his head or pierce his heart.

But it will take him far longer to heal from wounds inflicted by silver. And it will weaken him greatly. Enough for you to have a chance of capturing him."

"Where will we find him?"

"He has another secret office. It's where he keeps his own weapons."

"Show us the way."

I let him walk in front of us, the point of my blade pressed lightly at the base of his spine. He led us up the wide central staircase and along a series of passages until we reached a heavy wooden door. He tried the handle, and to my surprise it opened. The room was lit by a single candle perched on a desk, its flickering light causing a giant silhouette of Cornishe to dance against the wall behind him. He was rummaging around for something in his desk.

I pulled Filton behind me and told Rose to watch him while I approached Cornishe.

"You know what I've got here," I said. "A silver blade. No one needs to get hurt, if you'll just agree to come peacefully with us—"

Quicker than thought, Cornishe leapt up on top of the desk, squatting on his haunches, his arms propped on his knuckles. He snarled, his face dark with hate, then emitted a low growl that had nothing human about it. The hairs on the back of my neck stood to attention from a most base fear. He propelled himself forward at such speed I had no time to think. I lifted my blade, but Cornishe had by then struck me in the chest and knocked me to the floor. He landed beside me and then leapt again towards the exit, while in the same motion swinging his arm to reveal a heavy wooden club that missed my head by fractions of an inch and struck Filton's knees, knocking him across the floor. I instinctively swung at Cornishe with my sword. It was a lucky intuition; the silver blade connected with his thigh and his howl suggested it was more than a mere scratch. Blood oozed out from the wound and onto the floor, thick and dark as treacle. He let out another howl and then hurtled towards the doorway behind us, and before I could think of striking again, he was gone.

I rushed back out to the landing, but once again Cornishe was nowhere to be seen.

"He'll raise the alarm," I said to Filton. "If you can't help us, you're a dead man."

He got to his feet and held up his hands in defence. "You need to leave here if you want to survive."

"You don't understand," I said. "I need Joseph Cornishe. Unless I take a live lycanthrope back to my master, my life is not worth living. Now help me find him, or so help me, I'll kill you right here."

Filton paused for a moment. "Forget about Cornishe, he's too dangerous for you to tackle," he said. "If it's a lycanthrope you need, then there is another option."

"What?"

"There is another such creature nearby," Filton explained. "And we have him under lock and key."

(To be continued)

❧ 20 ❧

20th March 1766, Black Castle Estate, Westmoreland Parish, Jamaica

Cyrus sat upright. He was in a small compartment attached to the barn, on a floor of bare earth, with his back against a wall caked with mud. There was no room for him to take any other position, and he'd spent all the hours he'd been incarcerated in this same position. He couldn't even curl up, as his ankles were restrained by the bilboes: hinged iron rings attached to a long iron bar. His father had often threatened him with this punishment, but this was the first time he had actually followed up on it. It was a method of restraint normally reserved for the slaves who'd committed egregious crimes, such as stealing, or physical violence. His only relief was that they had not secured his arms.

There was nowhere for light to come in, so he could not tell what time it was. He measured the hours by the delivery of his food and water. Twice now Filton had opened the hatch, pushed a plate of gruel and a bowl of water across the floor before him. His father's house servant would always take a moment to gloat at his situation, before closing him in again without a word. Cyrus refused to look at him, but even out of the corner of his eye he could see the satisfaction Filton got from seeing him demeaned like this.

When Filton had arrived on the estate some ten years ago, he'd taken an instant dislike to Cyrus. This grew into something more like hatred. It was as if Cyrus had personally affronted him. Cyrus always assumed this was personal, a clash of personality intensified by the fact that his father gave him a special place amongst the inhabitants at Black Castle. But he came to understand it was borne from an intense disgust at his mixed race. The mulattoes in Jamaica seemed to instil different feelings in the whites. Most saw them as a middling race, a step up from the negroes but still way short of the respect due to other whites. But some deplored them even more than they hated the negroes. It was as if, by mixing white blood with black blood, the mulatto had transgressed some arcane law, some ancient myth of purity. Filton was one of these people, Cyrus was sure of it.

The third time the hatch opened, there was no bowl of gruel or water, just Filton standing there silhouetted by the moonlight. He pulled out a key and bent down to unlock Cyrus from the bilboes. As soon as they were free, Cyrus pulled his legs from the restraints and rubbed his ankles.

"It's your lucky day," said Filton. "There's someone wants to see you."

Cyrus frowned.

"Come on, up you get!"

Cyrus staggered to his feet and stumbled after him, trying to coax his legs back into the habit of moving. Even the moonlight looked bright after so much darkness, and his body ached as it struggled to regain its full memory of walking upright.

Filton led him across the grounds, but away from the house to the dirt track that ran alongside the main drive and away from the estate. There, waiting for them, were two strange figures, each on horseback: a white man in his early thirties, whom he'd never met before, and a young black girl with a striking face and sad eyes. The latter looked strangely familiar to him.

"This is he," said Filton to the white man.

The stranger glared at him. "My name is Captain Maddern. If you know what's good for you, you'll come with me."

They rode for more than an hour. Cyrus sat behind Rose on her horse, Filton rode with Maddern. Eventually, they came to a large building, which Cyrus recognised as the old hospital for the neighbouring estate. They dismounted, tethering the horses to the back of the building. Cyrus shuddered at the memory of this place, which they used to call the "hot house" because of its intense temperature. The sick and injured were treated, but slaves were given short shrift, and were severely punished if they were caught feigning illness to avoid work. Cyrus remembered the time he'd been sent here on an errand when he was just eight years old, and witnessed a slave boy of about his age arriving with a severed hand. The boy had been feeding sugar cane into the mill at the boiling house and had got his fingers trapped in the mechanism. His entire hand was crushed to a pulp, and another slave standing by with a machete had to hack it off at the wrist before his arm was drawn in any further.

The building had been out of use for a few years now. The main door was locked, but Filton had a key. Someone had clearly been looking after the place. In the long central ward, where previously there had been two rows of beds for sick slaves, there was nothing but a few armchairs, arranged in a circle. It looked as if it had been recently used for a meeting. Settling himself on a chair, Maddern beckoned everyone to take a seat and addressed himself to Cyrus.

"Young man, you clearly have more intelligence than others of your kind."

Cyrus winced.

"I want you to apply that intelligence now, and also to trust in me," Maddern continued. "This is of fundamental importance to your future. There are such things as lycanthropes: human beings that transform at the full moon into monstrous, wolf-like creatures. And your father is one of them."

Cyrus glanced between Captain Maddern, Filton and Rose. His father, a werewolf? Surely this was the stuff of legends and fairy tales. He weighed the possibilities. Perhaps Maddern was insane. Perhaps he'd killed his father and was trying to take the estate for himself. "What's happened to him?" he asked.

"We confronted him with his secret. Our intentions were honourable. I believe I may have discovered a cure for his condition, and I tried hard to get him to allow us to apply it. I'm afraid his reaction to this was hostile. At first he denied vigorously that he was indeed such a creature. When I told him we were here to help him, he objected that he didn't want our help and demanded we leave. When I pressed him further, he attacked. We were driven from the house."

"He attacked you?"

"Yes. His condition gives him unusual strength and speed, even when he's not in his werewolf form. You might perhaps have been witness to this in the past?"

Cyrus frowned. "I don't know," was all he could say.

"He has the strength of five, maybe ten men," Maddern continued. "And he is dangerous."

Cyrus saw it all with blinding clarity now. It was true. He knew it in his gut. But it went against everything he'd known about his father, everything he'd believed. Joseph Cornishe was a man driven by a core of righteousness. He'd always talked to Cyrus of the importance of responsibility, of putting duty above everything else. Duty to society, to elders, betters, rulers and governors. Cyrus despised him for it. What was he, Cyrus, to make of duty, after all? A half-man, born out of a white man's lust for a black slave girl. Cornishe had conjured his son out of this chaotic land. That put Cyrus at a disadvantage from the moment he was born. He had nowhere to fit, nowhere to feel safe, no one to call friend or family. Only his mother, and she'd died when he was too young to realise how much he depended on her.

"Do you know what this means for you?" Maddern said.

Cyrus glanced back up at him.

"Your position has become somewhat precarious. We could tell the authorities about your father. If he is captured, he will be exposed and dealt with by both the state and the church. Neither will be lenient. It is likely he will be tried and convicted, with a death sentence. This may be an age of reason, but we are not beyond burning witches and their kin at the stake. Without your father's protection, and with no living mother, you will become someone else's property. Now, I don't know for sure, it depends on your next owner, but I imagine this wouldn't be an outcome you'd welcome."

Cyrus felt the blood drain from his face.

Maddern let his pronouncements hang in the air for a few moments, as if to give Cyrus time to fully think this through. "Of course, there is another way. I have the power to give you your freedom. It's what you want most of all, correct? To be your own man, work for yourself, live independently, perhaps raise your own family? I can help you with this. But in exchange, I need something from you."

"What is it?"

Maddern stood up. "I haven't been entirely forthcoming about what I'm doing here. You see, I had a notion about your father's condition, thanks to my Obeah friend here." He nodded at Rose. "I've been seeking the creature for some time, although I didn't know its identity until last night. I am currently on a mission. It started many months ago, when I was engaged by an influential gentleman from England. This gentleman is also a bold and brilliant scientist, and he wants to learn the secrets of the lycanthrope. My confrontation with Joseph Cornishe this evening was the closest I've yet come to realising my mission. But now I've finally found the thing I've been looking for, it has slipped through my fingers. And then Filton here mentioned Cornishe had a son. You, Cyrus, are part of him, part of his bloodline."

Cyrus gazed at him. "I'm not a werewolf, I can assure you of that."

"No, you're not a werewolf. Not yet. But you do have the potential to become one. If you were conceived after your father developed his condition, then you are his heir in this respect also. You have the potential to develop lycanthropy, but it would require some sort of catalyst to make it happen. Or so I am told by our Obeah witch here."

"Like what?" asked Cyrus.

"Filton is the expert. But for my purposes, we simply want ..." Maddern paused and looked away.

"What is it that you want?" asked Cyrus, his clarity of thought returning. "I'm not a werewolf. What good can I possibly be to you?"

"We need your blood. If we can take a quantity from you, we can transport that back to my employer's laboratory in

England, and he will have everything he needs for his research."

Cyrus raised his eyebrows. "Since when has a white man sought permission of a black man to take his blood? You could have done this without my consent."

"It's not that simple. As I have mentioned, your lycanthropy is latent. For your blood to be of any use to us, we need it to be active."

"And how exactly are you going to make that happen?"

"We will need to activate your lycanthropy, just long enough for us to take a sample of your blood. As soon as we've done this, we will reverse the process, and you will go back to your normal state. And when we're sure you're well, and we have what we need ... you will be free. I will personally provide you with the means to start a new life. A small sum of money and a property here in Jamaica. For the first time in your life, you'll be capable of becoming what you want to be, and not what others want you to be."

Cyrus's heart pounded in his chest. Freedom was something he'd been willing to fight for, and here it was being offered to him for nothing more than a sample of his blood.

Maddern filled the silence. "We can't do this without your help."

"And if I refuse?"

Maddern smiled. "Well, we can't force you, of that I'm sure. What we are talking about would require your consent. If you chose to decline, you'd return to your current situation with nothing, and we'd have to continue our search elsewhere."

Cyrus nodded slowly. He glanced up at Rose and found her regarding him with a fierce intensity. Her high cheekbones and proud eyes seemed to hold a deeper mystery. He imagined her in another life, an African Princess, heir to a great warrior father.

Now he remembered where he'd seen her. She was the girl from his dream, he was sure of it. Was this his destiny being played out?

"When do you plan to do this?" he asked, looking back at Maddern.

"The full moon is in a few days' time," said Maddern. "We'll need to move fast."

22nd March 1766, Disused hospital, Westmoreland Parish, Jamaica

To Dr Melchior Croll, Bristol, England
   From Captain James Maddern

To summarise our situation: we have experienced good and bad fortune.

The bad fortune is that we let Cornishe escape. The good fortune is that his son is with us. A mulatto named Cyrus, born of a black slave woman here on the estate. The son is twenty-two years of age and it seems he knew nothing of his father's supernatural condition. The two of them have a fractured relationship, and the boy has no respect for the man. Cyrus has inherited his lycanthropy. All we need to do is to trigger and harness it. Filton has a conception of how to perform this initiation. He requires only the help of the Obeah, Rose, to put it into action.

We are at last on the verge of success. I will be bringing you back a specimen. When you have unlocked the secret of immortality I will get my Claire back, as I knew her, as I loved her.

You may wonder about the nature of this man, Filton, and how he has come to know so much about his master. It seems Filton was hired as more than just a manservant. He is a protector to Cornishe, and not the only one. Cornishe has established a network of associates on the island. Filton claims he has no knowledge of where the others can be found, but I don't believe him. I am keeping a close eye on him. So far he has co-operated with us, but only under duress. I've had to chain him up when we sleep, so that he doesn't try to overpower us or escape.

All being well, by the time you read this, we will have performed the rites that will turn Cyrus into the immortal form. We must do this here, apparently, as the earth on which he was born is a key part of the ritual. But we will secure him and ensure that he comes with us back to England in a docile state. Materials fashioned from pure silver will keep him confined and weakened, preventing his escape. I have everything back on the ship.

I know you will be excited by this news. Let us look forward from now until the day I return with the prize you so fervently seek.

Your faithful servant,
Captain James Maddern

22

23rd March 1766, Disused hospital, Westmoreland Parish, Jamaica

Cyrus awoke in a bed he'd made up in one of the rooms off the main ward, and reflected on recent developments. It was only a few days ago that he was travelling to the mountains with the aim of securing the aid of the Maroons and joining them in their fight against the white men. His fervour was already beginning to fade as he felt, for the first time, a sense of calm. He might have even called it satisfaction. With the money and means Maddern was about to give him, he would set himself up somewhere on the island. With this financial stability he would be in a strong position to free the black slaves, and make the white man pay for the horrors inflicted on his kind. And after Jamaica, the rest of the West Indies. And then Europe, America and beyond.

He also considered how Cornishe might attempt to get him back, and discussed this with Maddern.

"He won't let this rest, so we'll have to stay vigilant," Maddern told him. "After all, we've stolen his property."

Cyrus's stomach tightened at that. He didn't like to think of himself as Joseph Cornishe's son, but he was even less inclined to consider himself his 'property'. He tried to turn his attention away from the man. But the revelations took him back. All through his childhood, he'd had his suspicions. It was obvious, in retrospect. An incident came to mind now, one he'd never considered since it had happened.

He must have been around eight years old. It was a hot summer's day and he had been playing in the grassy area behind the house at Black Castle, when he thought he saw something large moving around up in the woods that bordered the plantation. He'd ran towards it to investigate, but as he'd reached the entrance to the woods he saw that there, sitting on the ground, was a ragged-looking white man. He'd resembled one of the white servants that worked on the farms, but was somehow different, dressed in rough garments, loose trousers tied at the waist and a dirty vest, with shoes that were worn to the point of being practically useless. And he'd smelt strange, a mixture of alcohol, smoke and something else, something that Cyrus had never smelt before, but that instantly nauseated him.

"Come here, boy," the stranger commanded. Cyrus noticed that the man pronounced words differently to any other Englishman he'd met. He may not have been English at all.

"I have to go home," Cyrus replied.

"Don't you want to see what I've got here for you first?"

Cyrus had known immediately that something was wrong. But hadn't experience taught him that to disobey a white man was a crime? "What is it?"

"Oh you'll like it. Just come and see. It's just in here."

For some reason Cyrus hadn't felt able to disobey. As soon

as he entered the shadows, the man grabbed hold of his shirt and pulled him down onto the ground.

"You are a pretty one, aren't you?" With his face close to Cyrus's, the smell was even more disgusting.

"No, no, no!" Cyrus's refusal ended in a shout. He wasn't sure what was happening, but he knew it was wrong. He'd been beaten a few times as a child, but this was something else. It was the first time he'd ever felt fearful for his life.

The man reached his hand up to Cyrus's neck and squeezed. "No more of your shouting, do you hear, boy?"

Cyrus gasped and tried to shout out again, but he couldn't make a sound. His face grew hot and his limbs went limp with the effort to resist. There was a horribly tightened expression on the man's face as he pushed his body hard against him. But whatever this man's intentions were, he never discovered. For the next thing Cyrus knew, his attacker was lifted into the air and thrown into one of the nearby trees. It was as if he'd been picked up by the wind, like a fallen leaf, and blown into the woods. He coughed hard, still shaking from the attack, and looked up to see his father striding towards the assailant, who was by now slumped like a scarecrow, his body twisted and limp. With one hand, Joseph Cornishe picked up the attacker by the throat and pinned him against the tree, his legs dangling a foot above the ground. Even at this age Cyrus had known this was a show of unnatural strength.

"Cyrus, get back to the house," commanded Cornishe over his shoulder. He showed no sign of physical strain, as if he were holding up a rag doll. What had impressed Cyrus then, and what he recalled clearly now, was his father's expression. His bright blue eyes seemed to have been lit from behind. Cyrus ran as fast as he could. All he heard behind him was the sound of a muffled scream and then silence.

As this incident came back to him, he realised he'd known

all along that Cornishe had a power beyond the natural. And with that certainty came an equally certain notion that Joseph Cornishe would find a way to punish his son for what had happened during this past week.

He made his way to the ward, where he found Maddern sat at a makeshift desk, writing a letter.

Maddern looked up and smiled at Cyrus. "In a few days you'll be your own man," he told him. "How does that make you feel?"

"It makes me feel ... vindicated," said Cyrus.

"This transformation ceremony is not going to be easy, you realise that?"

"Of course."

"I've been told how it works by Filton and the Obeah witch. I won't lie to you: it's going to cause you great pain. But consider the outcome."

"Freedom."

Maddern nodded. "And not just for you. I will be gaining freedom too, in a certain sense of the word. Our fates have been united, it seems. So, here's to liberty." Maddern lifted a goblet he'd been drinking from and tilted it towards Cyrus.

"Yes, liberty," replied Cyrus.

He had a lingering sense that something was wrong, but he pushed it to the back of his mind.

❦ 23 ❦

26th March 1766, Disused hospital, Westmoreland Parish, Jamaica

To Dr Melchior Croll, Bristol, England
    From Captain James Maddern

The ward of this old hospital is to be the location for Cyrus's transformation. I have learnt all I can from Rose about the ceremony. I knew you would want to hear everything about the procedure and I was more than a little curious.

The first thing she did was to create an Obeah shrine in the main ward. She explained it was vital we create a home for the supernatural spirit to join us. She placed a brass pan on a makeshift altar and filled it with dark and loathsome ingredients, explaining them thus: "This is the mud from the ground he grew up on. These are Obeah's sacred plants: bissy, fever grass, bark of odum, cerasee. Here is the dust from a root that crosses a road and the plant known as 'leaf of life'. Here is the blood of his father. I gathered it from the floor when you cut him in his office. Here is the bark of the bonsam dua tree, and here a flake of virgin gold."

She proceeded to pound these ingredients into a pan while uttering a dark and foreboding incantation: "Ta Kwesi, we call you from the darkness. Here we build your shrine so that you may appear to us and draw from this man his hidden life. Come to us from your place in darkness, below the moon, and allow the beast his freedom."

I watched her in morbid fascination, the hairs on the back of my neck rising. After she finished her incantation, she closed her eyes and bowed before the shrine. The whole scene brought to my memory the horrifying experience I'd had with the voodoo worshippers in Hispaniola, making my blood surge and my head spin. I shook my head and brought myself back to the present.

Rose had finished her preparations and was now on her feet. She turned to me. "Ta Kwesi requires a sacrifice before he will come to us."

I felt a sudden terror. "What kind of sacrifice?"

"Sheep or fowl."

This was some relief. "There are wild chickens in the woods near here."

"They must be young."

"Why?" I asked. The sight of the boy, his blood splashing across the floor, flashed before my eyes.

"The blood must be clean, pure, untainted. It is only the young who can give Ta Kwesi what he desires."

"I'll ask Filton to see to it. In the meantime, I need some rest."

"One thing I must tell you." Rose stopped me in my tracks. "You know, this boy, Cyrus, he cannot go back."

I looked at the ground. "Yes, I thought as much."

"Once we start this change, there is only one way to reverse it."

"And what is that?"

"His father must die for him to shed this curse."

"Why so?"

"There are only two ways for a man or woman to become a shape-shifter. First, inherit it from one already cursed. Unless he is born from the mating of two werewolves, the condition remains dormant. It will not fully pass on until the child accepts the blood of his father, in a magical ceremony like this. If this be done, then the child becomes a shape-shifter too."

"So if it weren't for this ceremony, Cyrus would never become a werewolf?"

"He would remain latent for all his life. The *Jé Rouge* is a magical creature. To inherit is a privilege. It is only for those who choose the path, and only when they come of age."

I confess my heart sank. I hardly know the boy, and I cannot concern myself with his fate. But one can't help but feel empathy for the poor creature. "He believes he will be free," I said to Rose.

"It is a curse and a blessing," she replied. "Three months after turning, it will be with him forever. But if, within that time, he kills his father ... then the bloodline is broken and the curse will leave from all his descendants."

"It is unlikely, then, that Cyrus will avoid this fate. His father will be difficult to kill, no?"

"A werewolf can be killed. Piercing through the heart or taking off his head. But that can only be achieved with a silver weapon. Even then, he can be revived. If his corpse is laid out under the light of the full moon, he will regain life. I was told by Obi that a severed head can be reattached and the werewolf brought back to life this way."

"Extraordinary. You mentioned another way for a werewolf to be created. What would that be?"

"The only other way is by the saliva or the blood from a shape-shifter, when he is in changed form, passing into the human's blood. Normally it is a bite that does it. If the human survives the bite of a werewolf, he becomes a werewolf himself."

I report all this to you, Melchior, but I have no way of knowing whether it is true. Maybe all of it is, maybe none of it. But so far, all I've heard is talk. I've seen their barbaric rites, but no proof that their black magic actually works. Cornishe certainly looked wild on the evening I confronted him, but there are rational explanations for such behaviour. However, here, this evening, I will see for myself whether a man can be transformed into a beast.

Rest assured, I made our intentions clear to Rose. "If what you say is true, we must contain him," I told her. "My job is to get this creature back to my employer in one piece."

And that I will do. I will write to you anon with news of our success. In the meantime, I remain your faithful servant,

Captain James Maddern

24

26th March 1766, Disused hospital, Westmoreland Parish, Jamaica

Cyrus peered into the ward from the side doorway. It was entirely transformed, lit up by dozens of candles around the walls. The chairs had been shifted aside and there was a cage in the centre of the room, in front of which stood Rose. The hood of a dark cloak covered her face. Her hands were linked in front of her and her head was bowed.

Cyrus was dressed only in a sackcloth taken from a store of clothes meant for the sick slaves. If this was leading to his freedom, why did he feel like a prisoner? "The cage?" he asked, looking at Maddern.

"That is for our protection," he replied. "You know what you will become. We have to keep you secure until you revert back to your human state."

"I understand," said Cyrus, scratching his throat.

"Now come, we must begin. Soon the full moon will be our

only light. According to the Obeah, this is the only time the ceremony will work."

Maddern led Cyrus to the cage, opened the door and gestured inside. Cyrus entered cautiously, then Maddern closed the door behind him and locked it with a heavy iron padlock.

It was a large cage, high enough for Cyrus to stand fully erect in, and wide enough for him to take several paces across.

"Do as she tells you," Maddern said, gesturing to Rose.

Cyrus looked up at her. She lifted the hood from her head to reveal her face, which was now painted with various earthy colours, red, brown and gold, on the cheeks and forehead. She had always looked otherworldly, but now she looked un-Godly. The sight of her sent a shot of lightning down his spine.

Rose started to intone a mystic incantation, beginning with the words: "Supreme being, upon whom men lean and do not fall ..."

Cyrus had no idea what these words meant, but there was something about the way they were spoken that produced a feeling of nausea deep within him. Rose continued to utter her spells for a minute or so, then paused and reached to the floor to pull a young chicken out of a box before her. She held it aloft in her left hand as she spoke again:

"We have taken a young one, a fowl, and we give it to you that you may come here to give life to the beast within this man."

With her free hand, she lifted a goblet from the table beside her and drank its contents.

"We have taken wine so that you may reside here and bring forth new life. O Tano's fire, today we have established your shrine on the full moon, so that you will become our God. Upon this sacred night we beg your assistance."

A knife appeared in her hand. She lifted the blade high up to the ceiling, its metal glinting in the moonlight that flooded through the window behind her. With a speed that shocked both Maddern and Cyrus, she slashed violently at the young chick. Blood gushed forth as she held its fresh, twitching body above the bowl. The chick's blood soaked into the dusty compound that she'd forged from the macabre ingredients. When the blood had finished dripping from its neck, she brought out a small glass vial and unstopped it. Inside was a thick black-red substance.

"This be the blood of this man's father," she said as she tipped the final ingredient into the potion. "May the line of the beast continue through him. May it bring forth the creature that lies sleeping in his blood."

Rose picked up the potion and advanced towards the cage. Cyrus looked at her, gripped with a terror he'd never experienced before. Rose stopped in front of the cage and proffered the potion through its bars.

"Drink all of this potion and become what your destiny demands of you."

Cyrus reached through the bars and took the vessel from Rose, who appeared transformed to him now into a fully fledged Obeah priestess. With the wine and the blood, the mixture had become a dark sludge. Its stench made his stomach lurch. He looked up again at Rose and then over to Maddern, who was still watching from the side of the ward. Maddern gave a barely perceptible nod of encouragement.

Without further thought, Cyrus grasped the vessel with both hands, brought it to his lips and took a sip. The concoction crawled into his mouth and down his throat like a giant centipede. The taste was unimaginably foul and it took every ounce of his strength to stop himself vomiting the substance back up again. Maddern watched him take it down with something like awe in his eyes.

Despite his involuntary heaving, Cyrus managed to take

the rest of the liquid into his mouth, but it was still a struggle to swallow. He was desperate for a cup of water to help it down, but his mouth was so dry now that he couldn't get a sound out, and Rose made no sign of offering him any aid. He could feel the odious potion travelling down his throat, slithering towards his stomach. When it finally got there, the impact was sudden and violent, an explosion under his skin, as if all the veins in his body were on fire. The pain was so intense that it seemed miraculous his skin and flesh were not melting from his body. He tried to scream, but the raw dryness in his throat made it impossible to form sounds, and he fell to his knees, clutching his stomach in wordless agony.

Then he passed out.

❧ 25 ❧

26th March 1766, Disused hospital, Westmoreland Parish, Jamaica

To Dr Melchior Croll, Bristol, England
   From Captain James Maddern

I could only look on in morbid fascination at the change that overcame Cyrus. After he drank the potion, his body became racked with devils. The sound! Skin stretching, bone cracking, limbs contorting. His back arched up in spasms and the bones clicked across the full length of his spine, as it twisted into its new shape. Hair sprouted all over his body like worms escaping a fire. He held himself up on all fours, his face twisted in the darkness, his mouth wide open, bellowing an agonised scream. And that was just the start! Next came the most violent transformation of all. His whole lower jaw shoved outwards, his teeth shunting outward to reveal a set of over-extended canines that grew as long as daggers. His nose burst outwards to form a large bestial snout, while his ears popped and snapped into their new wolven shape.

When Cyrus no longer bore any resemblance to the man he once was, the newly formed beast reared up onto its hind legs and let out a guttural roar that echoed around the room. I pressed my back against the wall. Here it stood, the beast we've been seeking, in all its dark glory. I had no presence of mind to think about the true nature of the miracle I'd just witnessed. Instead, my attention was captivated by the most horrifying, unearthly transformation I've ever witnessed. Standing well over seven feet tall, with claws and teeth as sharp as swords, it was the embodiment of evil, the essence of Satan himself. It had all the outward signs of a giant wolf, its dark brown fur tinged here and there with a deep red. But it had the bearing of a man. And something like a man's intelligence burned behind its icy blue eyes, similar to those of Cyrus the man, but now speckled with fiery sparks.

I got a good look at those eyes, too. Moments after the gut-wrenching pain of the transformation, the beast stood panting in the centre of the cage, its chest heaving like bellows. Its composure was disturbing. I had expected to see it go berserk, break into a wild frenzy. But instead it just looked around, as if searching for something. It stared at Rose for a few seconds and then turned its head towards me, sensing my presence even though I hadn't made a movement or a sound. I felt hypnotised by its power, and despite myself, I stepped from the shadows to get a closer look at the phenomenon. My eyes met the beast's, and it was as if the creature had known I'd been there all along. It was a savage face, but the eyes showed supernatural depth. There was the human element, but something else also. Something older and deeper. It was as if its eyes contained the whole history of its kind, of everything that had led up to the incarnation of this creature standing before me; as if it was merely the latest in a bloodline of immortals that stretched back to the beginning of time. That cold blue fire that burned in its eyes, like a frozen lake reflecting bright winter sunshine, shone into my soul like a gateway to infinity.

For the first time I understood why you sent me on this mission. This creature, this thing that had been the mulatto Cyrus, was now more than human, more than beast: it was a god. Not *the* God, of course not. But a deity from antique times, one that had become forgotten by mankind. I felt an overwhelming urge to kneel down and worship, to welcome its savage hunger and surrender to its appetite. Whether I lived or died no longer mattered to me as I stood contemplating the cosmos within the eyes of that beast. All that I desired was to be subsumed into that glorious vision.

The creature roared and pounced forward within the cage. Its weight was such that it thudded against the bars of the makeshift prison, and I fancied I saw them give. Such strength. That savage snarling would have been the last thing I'd have heard in this world if it weren't for those bars. The werewolf now sensed it was trapped, and prowled warily around the cage on all fours, before standing upright, throwing back its arms, pushing out its chest and roaring into the night.

The spell on me was broken, and now I struggled to control my physical reactions. When at last I felt capable of speaking, I turned to Rose, who had been standing calmly in front of the cage since the transformation.

"Are you sure he's safely enclosed in there?"

Rose nodded. Despite her proximity to the cage, the werewolf seemed to be paying no attention to her, but was instead fixated on me. "We must leave it be now," said Rose. "By daybreak it will turn back into the man you knew before this change."

I will report on any further developments as they occur. Until then I remain your faithful servant,

Captain James Maddern

❧ 26 ❧

27th March 1766, Disused hospital, Westmoreland Parish, Jamaica

Cyrus felt the light burning against his eyelids. He'd never felt the pain of daylight before, but now it rained down on him like fire from a volcano. He blinked, trying to take in the light without feeling the pain. His surroundings started to come into focus. Looking down, he found himself at the bottom of a cage. The sackcloth he'd been wearing was a pile of rags in the corner. The space around the cage was empty. He put his hands to the floor of the cage to push himself up and let out a grunt of pain, slumping back down. What had happened to him? He felt a searing ache right down to his core.

"Your bones will take time before they feel the same," said a voice from the edge of the room, beyond where the light from the sun was shining through the windows.

"Urgghh," blurted Cyrus. He'd meant to ask what Rose meant, but found his tongue and lips were just as broken as his limbs. The pain travelled swiftly to his face. He realised with that effort to speak that his throat was as dry as a cave and his tongue swollen. He pushed it around his mouth, trying to promote the saliva that would give him the moisture he needed to speak, but all he could feel were raw gums and the saltiness of his own blood. By now his eyes were watery with the effort.

"Do you know who you are?" asked Rose, as she stepped out of the shadows.

Cyrus lay still on the floor of the cage and looked up at her standing above him, silhouetted against the window.

"Here," she said, pushing a cup of water between the bars. "Drink this as soon as you can."

He became aware of a powerful thirst, like nothing he'd ever experienced before, but he could not reach for the cup. Every muscle and bone in his body howled and he knew that if he tried to move again, it would cost him more pain than he could bear. He thought he might die before he could move, but as soon as the thought came to him he realised that, no, there, humming in the background, behind his pain, was a power. It was a power he'd never been aware of before, but it also felt strangely familiar, as if it had been with him always, like an ancient memory, grabbed from his past and replayed in his present. It occurred to him that all of his life had been leading up to this moment.

As these thoughts fluttered through his brain, flashes of visual memory returned. He saw the violent images of the previous night's experience, stuttering between layers of darkness. He experienced again a vision of the room that swelled and exploded with new colours. Or rather something other than colour; a different kind of sense, mixed with heightened hearing, smell and taste. Blackness, and then another memory, this time of his body as a vessel, yes, a ship, roaring through the ocean, his lungs filled with the wind, like the tattered sails of some sea-borne war machine. Blackness, and again a snippet of memory: his arms like heavy branches, across his back a rush of fire, through his chest an expansion of heat, his breath panting like an engine of war.

"You must feed." Rose's voice once again wrenched him from his fantasy. "You will not feel like eating today, but you must. Otherwise the pain won't stop."

Slowly, painfully, Cyrus lifted his hand from beside him and groped forward to pick up the cup that Rose had laid beside his head. He lifted it shakily to his lips and tipped it down his throat. The fire in his stomach cooled and a strength rose up in him, like steam from a furnace. He gulped it down, every drop, and then lifted his head to speak.

"More," was all he could manage.

Rose brought forth a jug and tipped more water into the cup before pushing it back towards Cyrus. He downed this even faster than the first time and finally he was able to speak clearly.

"Get me out of here."

Rose gazed down at him solemnly. "Not yet," she said.

"We had a bargain," he croaked. "I've given Maddern what he wants."

"I'm sorry, Cyrus," said another voice.

He looked round to see Maddern walking through the brightly lit room towards him. He was hit by a sudden jolt, then another vision, a flash of colour, Maddern last night, the same Maddern but in his memory something other, too, something that called to his hunger. He fought to understand it, and then it came to him. He had wanted, more than anything he could ever recall, to sink his teeth into Maddern's flesh, to crunch his bones and tear his limbs apart. The shock of this memory electrified and disgusted him. He shook his head and brought himself back into the here and now. He felt his face tighten.

"We had an agreement," he said again.

"Things have changed," said Maddern. "You'll transform again tonight. And the night after. The three nights of the full moon. During this time, you're a threat to yourself and those around you."

Cyrus frowned. "You're going to keep me in a cage. You lied to me."

"In any case, you need to accompany me."

"I don't need to do anything."

Maddern nodded, his lips pursed. "Believe me, we have no choice."

"We? Who's we?"

"My benefactor. He needs to … understand you. He'll study you and then he'll let you go."

Cyrus chuckled, despite himself. "You really expect me to believe that it will be as simple as that? After you've already betrayed me?"

"You're not the prize, Cyrus. It's what you carry inside you that my master wants."

"He wants that beast? Why?"

"According to legend, you're immortal now. The secret of eternal life is within you."

Cyrus shook his head. "Immortal?"

"Please, believe me. It's not for us to understand."

Cyrus sighed. "Where is this benefactor of yours?"

"Bristol. England."

"Ha!" Cyrus spat. "So your plan is to ship me overseas? In a cage?"

"There are ways to keep you under control. You'll find you

have an aversion to silver. It's part of your condition. That's why you can't break through these bars. It weakens you. Now, you must rest. We have a long journey ahead of us. And we'll need you to be in prime condition when we get there."

At that he turned and left the room, leaving Cyrus to ponder his new fate.

❧ 27 ❧

28th March 1766, Disused hospital, Westmoreland Parish, Jamaica

The cage that contained Cyrus had been left in the old hospital ward until they could make preparations for the departure. Rose sat cross-legged on the floor, hands on her knees, eyes shut tight. Cyrus shook the bars of his cage until she opened her eyes. He'd been through two nights of transformation now, and his nerves were strained to snapping point.

"If you're going to keep me prisoner, you may as well tell me what I've become."

Rose pursed her lips. "You're a lycan now. Shape-shifter. Werewolf."

"Yes, but what does that mean?"

"It means that every month, for three nights when the moon is full, you turn from a man into a beast."

Cyrus nodded. "I can feel it within me. It wants to come out."

"The beast is always with you. He is part of you now."

"It wants me to kill."

"Yes, you must kill. Or go hungry."

"And I have eternal life?"

"The only thing that can kill you is a silver weapon. This is your blessing."

"You call that a blessing? It sounds like a curse."

"I think many people want to live forever."

"I just want to be free."

Rose looked away.

Cyrus felt desperate. "Can this be undone? Is there any cure?"

Rose seemed to be contemplating something. She looked around and then dropped her voice to a whisper. "There is one way, yes. If you can kill the one who turned you, before three months have passed, then the curse will be lifted. But after three months, there is no way back."

"The one who turned me?"

"Your father. It is his blood that made you what you are now."

"My father? I would gladly kill him, if I could only get to him."

"There is no chance of that."

"He's a coward. If he had any guts he'd be here to ..." Cyrus paused. To what? Protect him? Hadn't he just punished him for wanting his own freedom? Their hatred for each other was the only thing they had in common. He let out a deep sigh and closed his eyes. The irony hadn't escaped him that he was now more trapped than ever.

❧ 28 ❧

To Dr Melchior Croll, Bristol, England
    From Captain James Maddern

Our plan was to have left here by now, but circumstances have conspired against us. Curse these negroes, they have risen in rebellion. We had a visit from a passing Redcoat, an army man. He noticed the hospital building was inhabited and stopped to talk to us. I thought at first Cornishe's men had caught up with us, but it turned out he was merely scouting the area and felt compelled to warn us. He told us of escaped slaves and barbarity in the countryside and advised us to keep the place secured. But he also brought good news. The military forces on the island have been mobilised and they are already dealing with the worst of the fighting in the north west of the country. There is a unit coming to Westmoreland. Apparently, this parish has the highest risk of insurrection.

As a consequence I've had to barricade us in this building. It is most inconvenient. The Obeah witch is charged with overseeing Cyrus, who remains in his cage.

According to our visitor, the militia has also gathered reinforcements, in a most unlikely form. By all accounts they have sourced Spanish soldiers, would you believe – so-called chasseurs from Havana. They handle fierce hunting dogs, which have a reputation for savagery. Apparently, Spanish chasseurs are fierce but undisciplined. They have only confirmed their loyalty so long as they are paid (which is apparently enough to overcome their natural enmity to the English). Nevertheless, they have largely acted as they pleased on the journey from Havana to Jamaica. I was told they insisted on fighting anything that crossed their paths, incurring a bloody skirmish with a French schooner and even attacking a trade boat from Spain. The Redcoat said our own men were shocked by their hunger for violence and thirst for blood, but they had no choice other than to put up with this behaviour to secure their support against the Maroons.

By all accounts their dogs are even more fearsome. Cross breeds, a mixture of hounds and mastiffs, they have been specifically bred to be unnaturally fierce. It appears these animals were infuriated by their confinement on board ship, and once brought onto land, they filled the quiet streets of Montego Bay with their howling and whining. They were temporarily secured in the yard of a government building in the centre of town, because the noise they gave out was so terrifying to the locals. Meanwhile their handlers, the chasseurs, took over the local inns and drinking dens, getting drunk, starting fights and generally disturbing the peace.

Despite all this, it gives me some relief to know that the

militia has support. The slaves here aren't well armed, but the Maroons are clearly a formidable force. I hope that any disruption will be swiftly dealt with. God willing, I will soon be in a position to set sail for England once this is over, and then I will bring you back your prize.

I will write again soon with an update on the situation.

Until then, I remain your loyal servant,

Captain James Maddern

❦ 29 ❦

A persistent pounding noise woke Cyrus up. He looked up to find Rose still sitting nearby.

"What was that?"

And then a voice, bellowing, from beyond the main door.

"*We, the former slaves of the Black Castle estate, demand your surrender.*"

Cyrus jumped to his feet. He recognised that voice. "Neptune?" This was one of his father's slaves.

Rose looked at him quizzically.

The sound of hammering, heavy tools smashing against wood. A few seconds of silence, and then the shattering of glass. More shouts followed by a crashing noise. It sounded to Cyrus like the front door was down.

Cyrus grasped the bars of the cage. "You've got to let me out. This is our people, our fight."

Rose looked around anxiously. "Quiet," she said to Cyrus.

"I will deal with this." She disappeared out of the main ward and into the entrance hall of the hospital.

"Wait," hissed Cyrus, but she was out of earshot.

Cyrus strained hard to hear the movements of the rebels. He heard dull thuds and crashes. It sounded like furniture being overturned and objects being smashed. He wondered what Rose was up to. Was she alerting Maddern?

He scanned the area around him and spotted the one thing he needed: the keychain that would open this cage and allow him to escape. It was lying on the floor where Rose had sat, a good few inches beyond his grasp. He stretched his arm through the cage, and just as he did so, he felt a fire shoot through his veins. It was the pain of transformation he'd experienced the night before. He looked up and saw that, sure enough, although the sun had yet to go down, the full moon stood out against the deep blue sky like a silver coin.

"No," he muttered. "No, no, no!"

He felt his cheekbones stretching as the wolf within him forced its way to freedom. Through the pain he heard, as if from a great distance, shots being fired and more yelling.

And then silence.

The door to the main ward burst open and four slaves rushed in, wielding field tools and blades. They looked around in astonishment at the one-cell prison.

The man at the front stopped, stared at the cage. And then he laughed. "Look who is here."

Cyrus peered through the darkness. "Neptune!"

"The half-man."

"Neptune, you can't stay here."

"Ha. You think you can scare me now? You all alone, my friend. No father to save your skin this time."

"You don't understand," Cyrus replied. "Please, for your own sake, get out of here."

"No, this time you no understand. Our people rising all over the island. The Maroons on our side. This be our time. And this your last chance. Tell me, son of Cornishe: which side you on?" With this Neptune raised his scythe, and the other men around him cheered and lifted their weapons.

Cyrus fell to the floor, doubled up in pain. The transformation was coming upon him fast. He looked up with bloodshot eyes. "You don't know what you're dealing with."

Neptune must have seen those eyes flashing, glowing out of the encroaching gloom, as something made him pause. He shook his head. "No, my friend. The slaves are properly taking over here. Time is up."

Cyrus felt a heaving in his gut. He fell to the floor on all fours and looked back in desperation at the keys on the floor. Just as he did so, a delicate, bony hand lifted the keychain from the ground and threw the keys towards him. Instinctively, he reached out through the bars and grasped the chain in mid-air. Rose stood there, her arm still extended from the throw. She nodded to him, then ran past the rebel slaves and through the door to the entrance, slamming it shut behind her. Cyrus heard a bolt. She'd locked them in.

He scrambled to his feet and shoved the keys into the lock, trying to turn it while his fingers cracked from the stretching of bone and muscle. The four slaves were within one step of the cage, and they moved forward to stop his escape. With a monumental effort, Cyrus yanked the key in its lock and barged the door open. He was free, but the change was upon him. This time it was quicker than the first. His snout extending in excruciating pain, his arms and legs twisting into new shapes, coarse hair sprouting from his spine.

He looked up, pain contorting his features, blood filling his eyes. Neptune was frozen, eyes wide, as were the slaves standing with him. The fear had delayed their flight response just a fraction too long, and that sealed their fate. Cyrus leapt to his feet and pounced forward, landing a blow on Neptune with one arm, sending him sprawling to the floor, while grabbing another slave's head with the other. As Cyrus's claws ripped into the rebel's face, his scream triggered the remaining onlookers to run. They rushed towards the door in panic, scrambling over each other in their desperation to escape.

Cyrus held the slave's torn face in his hands and yanked the head from its shoulders, dropping the headless corpse to the ground. The other slaves were now frantically trying to open the door and escape. In just two strides, Cyrus was upon them. He tore at them with an instinct for the kill, and they fell to the floor lifeless, one with a gouged throat, the other with a punctured heart. Neptune lay dead on the floor by the cage. The last part of Cyrus the man was now consumed by the beast's appetite. His humanity fell away, but not before he witnessed his beast, feeding on the flesh of the rebel slaves.

❧ 30 ❧

28th March 1766, Disused hospital, Westmoreland Parish, Jamaica

His first thought was that he was dying. But then he realised the heavy pulse he could hear was his heart.

The next thing he knew was the hunger.

It burst through his skull with a manic energy that split him in two. Electricity shot through him in great surges. A shuddering, palpitating rush, his nerves and sinews twitching with orgasmic rage. Darkness enveloped him. And then, through the darkness, he glimpsed a world bathed in colours so vivid it was as if he was seeing them for the first time. Deep reds, vibrant purples, pulsating browns and yellows. A face screaming, and then the taste, the sweet, sweet taste of life. Life swimming in his mouth, gushing down his throat. Life throbbing in his gullet. Burning through his body, a gargantuan rush. A roaring, like an ocean, filling his ears. And then a cosmic uprising of blood that filled all his senses. Intense intoxication. His consciousness sagged with it, fell away, and rose up again, like a body thrown from a ship in a storm, to be tossed blindly on a struggling sea. He let himself be carried on that surge, a to-ing and fro-ing that brought him calm, then anger, darkness, then light.

He drank more life, swallowed it, drew it into his body.

And then an unbelievable shot of energy. Nerves awakened, as if they'd been dead since he was born. Sparks from his hands, feet, legs and arms shot through his system. He was running, jumping, springing. He was moving, and with that motion he became part of a new self, finding himself anew in the leaps, bounds and canters that propelled him forward, and out through a shattering and splintering of wood.

Now the colours were changing. Overhead were bright oranges and deep greens. The smells around him were new. The air hummed with a fresh vibrancy that filled his body with longing; longing for an unrestrained boundlessness, a freedom from the world, a freedom from himself. Now a connection of tissue and bone. A tense interlocking of joint and muscle. A oneness of soul, body and instinct.

He didn't will himself here or there; rather he felt himself free to wander, allowing his body to show him the way. If anything it was his hunger that drove him forward, that gave him the strength to move and the sense to discover. He was fully surrendered to it now, submitting to the unrelenting force of his nature, letting himself become what he needed to be to find his way. It was all pure action, but an action that observed itself, an action wrapped up in thought that made it all the more real and all the more free.

It wasn't the thought of freedom that came to him now, but the feeling of it. It felt as if every minute were a new awakening, every second a re-experiencing of the world afresh. He had an urge to scream and as this thought swam into his consciousness, he felt his throat stretch, his nose point to the sky and, from his gut, a deafening roar of victory, victory against life. A monstrous howl whipped out into the night and ricocheted across the clouds.

Something shifted around him, subtle at first, but then clearer and more perceptible. A distant scent, the whisper of a movement, the subtle displacement of molecules of air in one way, then another. He thrust himself back into the world, drawn now by a new sense of life. Not just his own life, but the life around him. The charged life of the trees and grass, the fearful, scurrying life of the animals that sheltered here, and the dark, devouring life of the creatures that ruled this land, familiar creatures he'd known in a previous life, or the dream of a previous life. He could sense their presence and it maddened him.

As he ran, the smaller creatures leapt from his path. They were quick, many of them too quick even for him. But they weren't what he was hunting. Across the forest, across the land, he could sense the bigger goal. A single body, stumbling, groping, battling through the dark forest, crashing into the edges of his senses. And another, something more akin to himself, alongside it.

He stopped, looked up, and then around. He could see through the trees, feel, rather, the presence of a man, with a canine companion. The dog sensed him too. But it wasn't afraid. Or rather, its fear was mixed with awe. It signalled a deference to him, through subtle signals, paw marks on the ground, low whines and yaps into the air. It guided him forward, through the trees, until he broke free of the dark foliage around him. Cyrus, buried deep beneath his wolf now, beheld the startled human before him. The man turned and looked at those eyes, and Cyrus felt his snout tighten and his legs tense. He felt his jaws clench and his saliva gather, and his claws strain and his fur lift. He felt his wolf leap forward, springing on those coiled muscles with so much ease it felt like flying, and landing right into the path of the human. He felt a reaching out, but fast, like a whip, and saw the head of the man in his wolf's giant claws. He felt his wolf's teeth sink into the neck, his wolf's tongue lap at the tendrils of sweet flesh. He felt the hot blood that poured down his cheeks.

The dog was barking, scared but steadfast. Cyrus's wolf wallowed in the corpse of his fresh kill, steeping its muzzle into the bloody ruins of the body and inhaling the remnants of the ripped flesh. Glorious feeding, overwhelming pleasure. He felt his wolf step back and draw breath, look down and see the shipwreck of a body, bones broken and skin torn, and then the hound, his companion now, was onto the man-flesh too, tearing and ripping.

They gorged themselves on human flesh, the dog driven by Cyrus's example. When they paused, the dog nuzzled its snout into Cyrus's fur. They rose as one and ventured further into the forest. Cyrus felt everything his wolf felt, and knew there was more to be done: more flesh to be taken, more blood to be drunk, more life to be consumed. He knew this hunger would never end.

They crashed through the trees together. There, in the clearing, was a group of maybe twenty soldiers, with four or five dogs. Cyrus felt his wolf's muscles relax for a brief second, and sensed his canine companion doing the same. Then they tensed and sprang together.

❧ 31 ❧

To Dr Melchior Croll, Bristol, England
  From Captain James Maddern

It is chaos here. The slaves are in revolt, in cahoots with the Maroons. They broke into the old hospital we're occupying and ransacked the place. I thought we were doomed. Filton and I barricaded ourselves into one of the side rooms and readied ourselves for the onslaught, but it never came to that. From what I could make out, the monster escaped its confinement and slaughtered them.

When we were certain the rebels were gone, we came out to survey the damage. Cyrus's cage was open, with no signs of breakage, so it must have been unlocked. We found the corpses of four slaves. If there were more, they must have scattered on seeing the monster. Rose, the Obeah witch, is nowhere to be found. She likely ran away in the confusion.

Dr Croll, I will do everything I can to find Cyrus and secure him again, have no fear of that. We can feel some confidence of finding him – after all, he has nowhere secure to go to. If he had any faith in his father, then perhaps he might seek him out. But no, there was never anything between them. His mentor, Tom Hartnell, is dead. He has nowhere to run.

Filton and I will see if the rebellion has been put down yet, and if there is anything we can discover of Cyrus's movements. We will have him back within days, I will make sure of it.

Until then, I remain your loyal servant,

Captain James Maddern

32

29th March 1766, Westmoreland Parish, Jamaica

Cyrus rolled to one side, trying to ease the crushing ache in his spine. He was awake now, but his eyes were still closed, and the pain throughout his body convinced him that if he tried, he would be unable to move. His first thought was that he might be dead, and that he was currently suffering in some afterlife of pure darkness. But then he was hit by the rich aromas: the freshness of the grass, the cooling trees and the pungent plants. It was as if he could 'see' with his sense of smell alone.

Then came the sounds. Not just the distant birdsong, but the swaying of leaves in the light breeze and the patter of tiny claws on the forest floor. He had never before experienced such a detailed awareness of his surroundings, and he was yet to open his eyes.

When he did look, he found himself lying curled at the bottom of a tree, in a small clearing, completely naked. He blinked, trying to regain focus. It was early morning, just after

dawn. He still couldn't move, but as he scanned the environment, he was shocked by the sight of the human corpse that
lay at the other side of the clearing. The chasseur's body was
stripped of flesh, down to the bone, half devoured. Cyrus's
initial horror soon abated as his hunger sharpened. There was
a sound just behind him. He spun round to find a large mastiff
lying beside him. It too was raising its head. The dog was huge
and its face was scarred. It gave him a lazy look, yawned and
licked its lips.

Cyrus stretched his limbs. There was a strength and a
vitality that flowed through him that he couldn't account for.
Indeed, he had no recollection what he was doing in this
situation and how he got here. His entire memory was
marred by a fog of indistinct images – distant, colourless
impressions. Things started coming back in more detail – his
capture, his imprisonment, the ceremony. And then, in
violent flashes, his own change. Vivid images burst into his
brain, and though he knew they were his memories, they
seemed to originate from somewhere outside himself, as if
they'd happened to someone else. Faces screaming, human
flesh tearing, dogs howling. Each lurid image filled his
thoughts with a savagery that, far from revolting him, gave
him a sense of freedom. Freedom from captivity, yes, but also
freedom from the shackles of humanity, morality and
restraint.

He felt a heavy breathing just behind his shoulder and
turned to find the dog's muzzle pressing close to his face. He
sensed that it was somehow deferring to him. A tongue lapped
at his face.

"Don't lick me," said Cyrus.

The dog tilted its head and whined.

"For Christ's sake."

Cyrus put his hand out to stroke the dog and found that

the animal had a collar on, with the name 'Leoncico' engraved on it.

"All right, Leoncico. What are we going to do now?"

Cyrus considered his nakedness. He wasn't going to get far like this. Maybe there was something he could salvage from the corpse. As he stood, his legs nearly buckled beneath him. Cramp shot through his muscles. Leoncico looked up at him with concern, and he steadied himself by holding on to the dog's back. He took a deep breath and dragged himself upwards into a standing position. The soft part of his feet flexed on the ground and he felt the energy of the nature around him travel up and into him.

As his strength returned, he took some tentative steps over the clearing to get a good look at the dead chasseur. The man's head and torso were in a considerable state of ruin. Great chunks of flesh had been torn from the upper half of the body and the face had a terrifying, twisted aspect, as if frozen by the sight of the devil himself.

Cyrus was in luck. Despite the terrible damage above the waist, the man's pantaloons were intact. He tugged at the bottom of his legs to pull the clothing free. In a moment Cyrus had secured himself something to cover his lower body. The man was a little shorter than Cyrus, so the bottoms flapped around his calves, but it was better than nothing. He turned back to see Leoncico nosing the corpse's bare legs, perhaps looking for more food.

"Come away from there," snapped Cyrus. It occurred to him that it was he himself who had caused the destruction to this poor wretch, rather than Leoncico. Who was he to deny the dog his portion? Leoncico sniffed at the corpse, then grasped a chunk of thigh between his teeth and ripped it from the man's bones. Cyrus wondered if the corpse was Leoncico's last owner. It spoke of poor loyalty if so, but then maybe this was part of the process, marking a change of allegiance. He realised he was watching the dog feed with an increasing hunger of his own. Although the thought of human flesh didn't appeal to him in human form, it didn't revolt him either.

"Come on, we've got to get going. I'm sure we'll find more food on the way."

With nowhere to run, Cyrus wondered where they should go. He didn't allow himself to think of the curse he'd been blighted with now. That would have to wait. Whatever he'd become, he'd need to find out more before he could fully comprehend what it meant to his life and how he could possibly cure it. The only man with answers to those questions was his father. And possibly Maddern, the man who'd captured him. He wasn't inclined to see either of those people again.

And what of Rose? Hadn't she given him the key to help him escape? She might be the only person he could trust.

He looked back at Leoncico and nodded his head eastwards. "We're going to Savanna la Mar."

❧ 33 ❧

29th March 1766, Disused hospital, Westmoreland Parish, Jamaica

To Dr Melchior Croll, Bristol, England
    From Captain James Maddern

We followed a trail of blood that led from the hospital to the nearby woods – the blood of its victims. At the woods, it had struck again. We found corpses, six of them, all fallen close together. I am guessing they were surprised by the beast and were unable to defend themselves. They were made up of English military and Spanish chasseurs. All of them ripped to pieces.

When we stepped into the woods I heard a sharp intake of breath nearby, and on closer inspection found a soldier cowering behind some foliage, his head in his hands, tears staining his cheeks, but unharmed. I pulled him to his feet and demanded he tell me what he knew, and after some gibbering and stuttering, I got the story out of him. He told of a giant creature that attacked his unit. He said it was dark and difficult to make out, but he was sure it was either a bear or some mammoth demon.

I brought him back to the hospital to interrogate him further. His unit and the Spanish had come to fight the rebels, accompanied by the infamous dogs. From his account, the emergence of the werewolf had caused terror and confusion. Soldiers scattered in all directions, but he was frozen with fear and watched as his comrades were torn to pieces by the monster. Most curious of all, the dogs deferred to the creature, probably recognising some arcane canine bond. The most fearsome hound in the company turned on its Spanish masters and fought alongside the werewolf.

The good news is that the rebellion is already being quashed. On my way back to the hospital I came across a messenger who was on his way from Montego Bay to inform the estates in this area that most of the rebellious forces had been put down. I gave him a description of Cyrus, but he'd seen or heard nothing of him.

Apparently, on the Black Castle Estate there were rebels, but most of the slaves were faithful and resisted the rebellion. The rebellious slaves are either dead at the hands of the beast, or killed by the English soldiers and Spanish chasseurs.

I have alerted the authorities to look out for an escaped mulatto slave. We will stop at nothing to get him back. I will keep you informed of all progress.

Until then, I remain your loyal servant,
Captain James Maddern

34

30th March 1766, Westmoreland Parish, Jamaica

The walking was gruelling, the heat overbearing, but Cyrus was determined to make headway before Maddern, or the law, caught up with him. He felt a new strength inside him, surging to the surface, driving him on. Everything about him felt reborn. His muscles ached, but they ached from an excess of strength. His blood felt like fire, and there was a quickness and lightness to his stride that gave him confidence in his ability to endure.

Leoncico trotted beside him. A bond had been forged between them, and it was as if they'd known each other all their lives. It was a silent bond, wholly impossible to articulate, but Cyrus kept a running commentary with his companion. It helped him feel as if he were bringing their kinship into the human realm. And he sensed that Leoncico was responding to his voice.

While he walked, Cyrus considered his options. Rose had told him his only chance for a cure was to kill Cornishe, but it had to be within three months. He couldn't go back to Black Castle Estate right away, though. It was too dangerous. For now, he thought only of Savanna la Mar. He could get there before sundown as long as he wasn't waylaid. Maybe Harold would help him again.

But what about Maddern? Would he think to look there for him too? Cyrus had no choice but to risk that.

Leoncico let out a volley of barks. Cyrus looked up to find that the dog was eyeing a noble-looking native, dressed only in cotton pantaloons and dark sandals. He wore a bunch of necklaces made up of bones, feathers and symbols, and his long black hair was gathered at the back of his head into a ponytail that hung down his back.

For a moment the three of them stood facing off across the space between them. After what seemed like an eternity, Cyrus took the first step.

"My name is Cyrus, and this is my dog, Leoncico."

The man nodded sagely but didn't reply.

"We're on our way to Savanna la Mar."

Still no response. He took some time to take in the man's appearance and noted that, while powerful, his upper body was also heavily scarred. It occurred to Cyrus that he was probably hungry, possibly desperate.

"Have you eaten?" he asked.

The man tilted his head slightly as if trying to comprehend.

"We've got some food here we would share with you, if you can help us."

The man looked cautious. Cyrus approached him and extended his hand. The man looked at it for a second and then took it in his own, curling his thumb around the palm and giving Cyrus's hand a firm grasp.

"You're welcome to join us," said Cyrus, wondering now if the man was mute.

"Join you?" came the reply.

"So you understand some English. We have no money. No money." He mimed open palms. "But I think we will have more success as two rather than one."

"Three," said the man, nodding towards the dog.

Cyrus nodded. "Yes, three. Well, this is the way we're going." He gestured towards the road again and detected a slight nod from his new companion. As he and Leoncico moved back towards the road, the man followed.

For the first mile or so they walked in silence. He had a strong feeling that this was a man who could be trusted. Leoncico also seemed at ease. A few minutes passed before Cyrus asked him, "What is your name?"

The man looked at him sternly, as if this were an important question. "White men call me Arawak."

Arawak. Cyrus recognised this as the name given to the original inhabitants of the West Indies, who had lived there for thousands of years before the Europeans. They'd been written and talked about by the historians of Jamaica, but the vast majority had been wiped out a long time ago, after the first Spanish settlers had colonised the area.

"Are you of Arawak heritage?"

"My great fathers were. But they dead long time. My mother, she come from the sea." He pointed out towards the ocean.

"So you are of two races," said Cyrus.

They were silent for a while.

"What you do in Savanna la Mar?" asked Arawak.

"I don't know yet. What about you?"

"Look for work."

They both fell silent and Cyrus could think of nothing

more to say. He looked away over the plains. It was going to be a long journey.

35

31st March 1766, Savanna la Mar, Jamaica

The markets were bustling in Savanna la Mar. A crowd had gathered in one of the squares to watch the slaves being brought out from the boats and sold at auction. By now it was late, and some of the spectators were drunk. What struck Cyrus most was the diabolical condition of the slaves coming off the boats. They were disorientated, weak and severely sickened. Their confused and pain-racked faces gave him a profound sense of impotence as he thought about their fate and his inability to help them.

Arawak looked on impassively for a short while, then turned to speak to Cyrus. "We go find work." He motioned towards the markets.

"Yes," said Cyrus. "Good luck."

Arawak stood looking at Cyrus and Leoncico for a moment, then disappeared into the market.

"Come, Leoncico," said Cyrus. "We need to talk to Harold."

Night was descending, and he knew that the longer he stayed here, the more danger he was in. Maddern had told him he was a valuable asset for his master back in England. He may have alerted the authorities to his escape, and Cyrus faced the very real danger that someone might recognise him. Plenty of tradespeople in this town knew him by sight and would be under the impression he was the murderer of Tom Hartnell. No, he couldn't hide here for long.

His thinking was interrupted by a commotion from across the street. In a narrow alley between tall merchant houses, a group of six men were grappling with someone. Cyrus fought the urge to interfere, knowing he already had enough problems of his own. But that didn't stop him edging towards the commotion. As he got closer he could see that two of the men had hold of a slave girl. They'd pinned her to the wall. The girl was struggling.

"Stop," barked Cyrus.

The man who had hold of the girl was stout and brutish. His face was wide and flat, and his thick neck was hardly distinguishable from his shoulders. He turned around to see who had made the call. "Fuck off," he grunted.

"Leave her alone, she can't harm you."

"Will one of you lot get rid of this cunt!"

Three of the men advanced towards Cyrus. He tensed up, muscles straining, the hairs on his back rising. He heard the low growling of Leoncico by his side. The dog struck first, flying from its haunches, jaws wide open. The dog's weight brought the man to the ground and before he knew what was happening, Leoncico's jaws closed on his face. Cyrus struck out at the second man, grabbing him by the hair and throwing him to the ground face down like a ragdoll, then stomping on the back of his head. He felt the crunch of the man's nose as it broke against the solid ground.

The third man hesitated, giving Cyrus more than enough time to lower his shoulder and charge him in the stomach. The man folded instantly into a ball on the floor and Cyrus kicked him in the head three times in swift succession before realising that he'd knocked him unconscious. He now became aware that in his strength was something new. It reminded him of his bestial state, and although he wasn't in wolf form now, he could feel that new strength in his human form.

With these three out of action, Cyrus strode towards the remaining three men in the alley. He reached out to slam the leader's head into the wall, crushing his forehead like a melon. He threw him to the ground and faced the other two. One of them threw a punch towards Cyrus's jaw. Cyrus was surprised how slow this appeared. He easily sidestepped the punch and swung his own fist into the man's stomach. It was a strong stomach, formed of hardened working man's muscle, but Cyrus had put everything into his punch. His target staggered back against the wall and slid to the floor, gasping to catch his breath.

Cyrus sensed something behind him. This was a new sense, as if he could detect movement without sight or sound of it. He turned and grabbed the arm of the man who was about to hit him across the side of the head with a brick. As he held it, he noticed a knife flashing in another man's hand. Even he didn't have time to twist away from this in time. Fortunately for Cyrus, Leoncico reappeared, knocking the man to the floor.

Now two of the men were unconscious and two more were groaning on the ground from the blows they'd received. The others had fled. Cyrus stood above those who were still conscious, his fists clenched, while Leoncico stood over his victim, teeth bared, as if awaiting the order to attack. Cyrus stepped forward and lifted the brutish leader to his feet, as easily as if he were picking up a sack of sugar. "You're lucky we didn't kill you. If I see you again, you're dead."

He shoved him away and motioned for Leoncico to let the other go. They stumbled away, breaking into a run as soon as they found their feet. Only now did Cyrus turn to look at the victim.

"You?"

Rose looked up at him. "Cyrus?" Her face was tired, ragged. A single tear track ran across her cheek.

"Wait," said Cyrus, "are you here with—"

"No," she cut in. "He's not a good man." She looked around her, as if in a daze.

Cyrus reached towards her and slipped his arm over her shoulder. "Are you hurt?"

She shook her head.

"Come with me," said Cyrus. "We have to get out of here."

⚜ 36 ⚜

31st March 1766, Savanna la Mar, Jamaica

Cyrus sat outside the church in the square. The organ was a battered old machine, the organist an ageing, ham-fisted performer. He was playing a hashed version of Bach's *St Matthew Passion*. Cyrus recognised the melody from his youth. His father had often played him pieces by Bach on the piano at Black Castle. His father was not a great musician, but even he would have made a better job than this.

The morning was cool and bright. Cyrus turned to Rose. "Why did you save me?"

She tilted her head, confused.

"Back at the estate. When Neptune had come to take me, you let me out of the cage."

Rose looked at the ground and bit her lip. "I never wanted to be with that man."

Cyrus nodded and cast his eye over the square. He'd missed

it here. The busy merchants rushing to and fro; the more refined gentlemen talking of money and commerce; the servants and slaves, suffering and skulking and taking their time wherever they could. That was the great diversity here, all aspects of life. Apparently, this was nothing compared to London, Paris, Rome. Not for the first time he had an urge to leave this place, to travel across the water, see the old world.

Right now, though, he had a more urgent mission: to rid himself of the curse that his father had inflicted on him. He must make him pay, with his blood. But how? He needed information, and the only place he knew to look for that was at the Shark's Head.

"I need to talk to someone," he said to Rose.

She looked at him blankly.

"And I'd like you to come with me."

She turned away, looking back into the town. For a brief moment he expected her to refuse. Then she sighed.

"I think you'll need all the help you can get. And to tell truth, I have no better option right now. I'll stay with you. Until something better comes up."

For the first time in a long time, Cyrus smiled.

The Shark's Head was open for business already, and it wasn't yet midday. Before Cyrus had even opened the door, he heard the noise within. As he and Rose entered he saw them, a group of seven or eight gentlemen, upper-class types, entitled, enough so that they didn't care who heard them. From the look of them, they were fresh off the boat. They would have travelled in the best possible conditions: large cabins, full-sized beds, shielded from the realities of the sugar and tobacco trade that their investments powered and that secured them their wealth. They wouldn't be here long. A stop-off on their journey around the world, checking in on investments. Right now, there was no better investment in the world than the sugar trade of the West Indies. The triangular route was perfectly efficient. Ships sailed from Bristol and Liverpool to Africa, where they dealt in slaves, exchanging cheap goods for human lives. From there they'd drag their human cargo to the West Indies, to sell them to the landowners of Jamaica and Barbados. And from there back to England, bringing the sugar that was harvested on the plantations to feed European tastes.

Cyrus had never been to England, but he'd read about it in books. The lives they lived there were fantastical. Dinner parties, social gatherings, a leisurely life that gave them nothing to think about but the fluctuations in their wealth. These people were truly free, free to fall in love or pursue their passions. There was too much work to be done here in Jamaica for any such luxury. Of course, the big Jamaican houses saw their fair share of social events, parties and balls. But most people on this island were far too busy getting on with the work at hand. And his father, Joseph Cornishe, had shown no desire for the 'blaze and tumult of public life', as he'd once put it. He'd always been a withdrawn man, shunning society to indulge his own company. He would spend hours in his study, well into the night.

As far as Cyrus knew, Cornishe had never taken another lover, and certainly nothing close to a wife, since his affair with the slave girl, Lucy, Cyrus's mother. Had he loved her? He had never harmed or threatened her. He'd even shown some affection towards her. But she was never fully integrated into Cornishe's life. She remained living and working with the house slaves all through her short life and never knew the luxury of a soft bed or fine silverware. She'd died when Cyrus was a boy and Cornishe hadn't even attended her burial. Cyrus could picture himself, still, on the edge of the pit that swallowed his mother's body.

Cyrus looked away from the rich men and towards the bar, where Harold stood wiping glasses, as if he'd done nothing else since he'd last seen him. His head was tilted downwards, but he looked up to see Cyrus and showed no surprise at his presence. It was almost as if he'd expected him.

"Look who it is," said Harold. "Did you manage to save the world?"

"Take a seat here," Cyrus said to Rose. "I won't be a moment."

He darted forward, placed his hands on the bar and sprang over it with ease, landing inches from Harold's face. Before the innkeeper could blink, Cyrus had his hands around his throat and had picked him up off the floor. Harold dropped the glass he'd been wiping and it smashed on the floor.

Behind him Cyrus heard one of the voices from the table. "Confounded dogs are fighting! I say, boy, stop that, or I'll come over and whip you myself."

Cyrus glared at the table, his eyes ablaze. The gents had turned away, though, and hadn't noticed the wild-eyed mulatto. He turned back to Harold.

"You need to help me get to my father."

Harold gasped, trying to utter something, but Cyrus's grip was too firm. He waved his hands in a kind of surrender and Cyrus lowered him to the floor. When his feet were back on the ground, Cyrus relaxed his grip but kept his hand around his throat.

"Tell me you'll help me or I swear I'll choke the life out of you."

"I don't think you'll need my help," Harold replied.

"Why?"

"Because I've found you first." The voice came from behind him. A familiar voice. One that he'd known and hated his entire life. His father's face emerged from the shadows.

"What are you doing here?" was all Cyrus could say.

"I've come to rescue you, Cyrus. You're safe now."

❧ IV ❧

37

31st March 1766, Westmoreland Parish, Jamaica

To Dr Melchior Croll, Bristol, England
    From Captain James Maddern

I have let two lycanthropes slip through my fingers now, and I am determined to put right this wrong. I know I won't have a chance of seeing Claire again without an immortal to bring back to you. And you know well enough that without her, I have no desire to live at all. I can't approach Cornishe again. But I can attempt to track down Cyrus. It occurred to me the servant Filton would be a vital asset, especially now I've lost the Obeah girl. Filton has been compliant so far, but his loyalties lie with Cornishe. I had a frank discussion with him and explained he had two options: either come along with me and help me secure Cyrus, or die alone here in this old hospital. He chose the only sensible option.

Filton convinced me our destination should be Savanna la Mar. This is the only place Cyrus knows, outside of the Black Castle Estate. It's true he's wanted there for the murder of Tom Hartnell, his mentor, but he also has other associates in the town who might provide the support he needs to avoid capture.

Before leaving I paid the soldier we questioned earlier, tasking him to take a message to my crew on the Black Prince in Montego Bay. I've asked them to bring the ship to meet me at Savanna la Mar. We'll need to set sail from there as soon as we have recaptured Cyrus.

One of our two horses was missing (Rose must have taken it), so we had to ride together on the other, under the cover of darkness to reduce the possibility of being apprehended. A few miles out, we came across some woods that would afford us shelter and rest. I lit a fire and cooked meat for us both, and while we ate, I asked Filton to tell me all he knew about the history of Cornishe's lycanthropy. He drew his knees in close to his chest, as if nervous of sharing these secrets. But after a few moments' silence, he started.

"No one knows where the werewolves first came from," he murmured, his face barely visible in the darkness. "There have been reports of them going far back into antiquity, and wolf-men inhabit legends from China to Norway. According to the Society of the Wolf, the order I serve, it was Christopher Columbus who first brought them over to the new world. When that great Italian explorer first approached Jamaica he attacked the natives, the Arawak Indians who inhabited the islands. You will find it written in the histories that Columbus landed and 'loosed a savage war dog that bit their naked skin and did them great harm'. These same history books will tell you that these were hunting dogs, the same large mastiffs that had been employed by the Spanish military against the

Portuguese and the Muslims. There were certainly some of those on board. But one witness said he saw a dog tear apart one hundred Indians. Even the great mastiffs weren't capable of that kind of damage. No, they were led by a lycanthrope, a werewolf who had been captured in the Celtic lands and somehow coerced into the bidding of the imperial explorers.

"The strongest of the Indians was a noble young warrior named Guatiguaná. He fought bravely during the battle but was bitten by the werewolf and left for dead. His body remained on the battlefield, amongst the rotting piles of flesh and bone. What the invaders never realised was that he had somehow survived the attack. As is the way with this curse, his wounds led him to become a werewolf. He recovered and returned to what was left of his people, the small rabble of lost and forsaken natives who had avoided death at the hands of the Europeans. With his miraculous recovery and newfound power, Guatiguaná became their leader. He grew in strength and led the survivors into the wilderness to form a secret sect, the first manifestation of the Society of the Wolf."

"Why would they serve a werewolf?" I asked.

"It was like a religion. They believed the werewolf was a descendant of the gods, and his power passed on to their tribe. As they saw it, their service to this god would render them great rewards in the afterlife. Today, the higher order in the society are descendants of those who served Guatiguaná himself."

"What, is Guatiguaná no longer alive?"

"He disappeared around one hundred years ago, during the battles between the Spanish and English. An English force had been sent to the West Indies by Oliver Cromwell. When they got to Jamaica they defeated the Spanish, some of whom fled to the north, including Don Cristóbal Arnaldo Isasi, the last Spanish governor of Jamaica. He led the guerrilla troops who confronted the English invaders. At this time, the Society of the Wolf allied themselves with the Spanish, based on their joint fears of English rule. Guatiguaná fought alongside Isasi, but they were outwitted by the English commander, General D'Oyley, and defeated at the Battle of Rio Nuevo."

Filton paused in his narrative and looked away. It was dark, but I swear I saw a single tear spill from his eye. I wondered at his own reasons for serving the Society, but now didn't seem like the best moment to ask.

"The Society continued to operate under English rule, despite the loss of Guatiguaná. Following their support of Isasi, they became aligned with various foreign interests – first the Spanish, and later the French."

Filton looked at me, as if becoming aware of my nationality.

"You have to understand that English rule was brutal. Slaves were treated abominably, and the white servants were slaves in all but name. The Society recognised that life had been much better on the island under the Spanish. They made guerrilla raids against the English, and supported any antagonists who sought to displace them. They might have done it too, but for the fact that the English have a great skill for generating wealth." He smiled up at me. "And not always by honourable means. When Sir Thomas Modyford brought his settlers from Barbados and became governor, he chose to support robbery, rape and plunder in the cause of imperial expansion. The likes of Captain Morgan and his buccaneers thrived, and Port Royal became a Babylon of the modern age. Until the gods threw down their justice, and that city was swallowed up by the sea during the great earthquakes." He paused and looked at the ground.

"So at this time there was no longer a werewolf amongst them?" I asked.

"No. They served the memory of Guatiguaná and the Wolf God he represented. Some say he still lives over the sea and will one day return to free his people. But much changed with the arrival of Joseph Cornishe. He came to the island nearly twenty years ago and brought his lycanthropy with him. His is the Teutonic variety. A strain from the North of Europe, directly descended from the Vandals and warrior kings of Germany."

"How do you know all this?"

"The Society gathered knowledge over the centuries. There are books, arcane volumes, stories passed down verbally. They were able to identify his breed. He belongs to one of the most powerful werewolf strains on Earth."

"How did they discover him?"

"I don't know how it happened. Perhaps *he* discovered *them*. In any case, they found each other, and at last the Society had a new werewolf to worship. They saw him as the embodiment of their Godhead, the second coming of the Wolf God. They were sworn to protect him."

After this, Filton changed the subject and offered no more information on the werewolf guardians. We will rise with the sun tomorrow and find our way there.

I remain your faithful servant,

Captain James Maddern

❧ 38 ❧

31st March 1766, Savanna la Mar, Jamaica

"Don't lie to me!" Cyrus raged.

"I have no time for this," Cornishe replied. "I've already told you, my primary concern was to find you."

"Yes, to save yourself."

But it made no sense. If Cornishe had an agenda, what could it be? Did he know that Cyrus wanted him dead?

"How did you know I'd been turned?"

Cornishe sighed. "I felt it."

Cyrus tutted and turned his head away from his father. They were in a dark corner of the Shark's Head. Rose glanced over from her table, with a look that seemed to say 'do you need any help?' He shook his head.

Cornishe noted it. "You like her, yes?"

"What? I mean, she's helped me out. If it weren't for her, I would still be in a cage at the old hospital. Or on my way to England. Why did Maddern want to take me there, anyway?"

"That I don't know," replied Cornishe, thoughtfully. "Did he say anything to give you an inkling of his purpose?"

"I picked up bits and pieces. Something about his mentor back in England being interested in the existence of a lycanthrope. I gather the whole reason he was here was to track down a werewolf. And now it looks like he's found one. Or two, rather."

"Yes, but both of them have slipped through his fingers, no?"

Cyrus nodded. "I imagine this Croll fellow will be disappointed."

Cornishe closed his eyes. When he spoke again, his tone was hushed. "Melchior Croll."

"That's right, Melchior Croll. You know of him?"

Cornishe stood abruptly and paced the floor, an impenetrable look on his face.

Cyrus looked on in astonishment. "What is it? Tell me."

"Croll," repeated Cornishe. "It's ... someone I used to know."

"From England?"

"Yes."

"Friend? Or foe?"

"A bit of both," Cornishe replied. His eyes were staring into the past.

"And he knows you're a werewolf?"

"Well, yes. But he never knew that I came here, to Jamaica. Anyway, that was over twenty years ago."

"He's after something that will give him eternal life."

Cornishe bit his lip. "The fool! It's a curse."

"He wouldn't be the first person in history to crave immortality."

Cornishe sat back down and stared at the table, his chin in

his hands. "There's more to it than that," he said, as if to himself.

Cyrus wanted to know more, but he wasn't sure whether to ask.

"Well, whatever his motives, we have to stop him," said Cornishe.

"Why? Surely we should get as far away as possible?"

"No, he's spent the last twenty years looking for me and he won't stop. We must go to him."

"Ha," said Cyrus. "And exactly why would I want to do that?"

"It's not a question of wanting to. It's a question of needing to."

"Pardon me?"

"Do you want to remain in this condition?"

"Of course not."

"Then this is your only hope."

"That's not what I heard."

Cornishe glanced up at him. "And what have you heard?"

"Never mind. You tell me your plan."

"I'm thinking," said Cornishe. He stared at the table, deep in thought.

Cyrus soon lost patience. "Well, tell me what you think he can do for my condition, at least."

"He's been working on a cure."

"How do you know?"

"Because I was the one who initiated it. It was back in 1742. I returned from Europe to England with the curse. He vowed to help me."

"And so why did you come here?"

"I found out about his real motives. I needed to leave."

"But if he hadn't created a cure when you left him, what makes you so sure he will have one now?"

"I'm *not* sure. But he has been working on it for two score years. His is a fearsome intellect, the greatest I've ever known. If anyone is capable of solving this, it's him. He is our only hope."

"*Our* only hope?"

"You think I want to remain like this?" Cornishe's eyes shone in the low light. There was something in his gaze Cyrus had never seen before. "We're going to have to work together for the good of both of us. Understand?"

Cyrus decided to keep to himself what he'd heard about the bloodline. He had his father right where he needed him. He could play along with this plan of his until the time came to act. And if there was no cure by then, he would see an end to his father once and for all.

"I said, do you understand?"

Cyrus nodded. "Where do we start?"

"We start right here, in Savanna la Mar."

❧ 39 ❧

1st April 1766, Savanna la Mar, Jamaica

To Dr Melchior Croll, Bristol, England
    From Captain James Maddern

Filton and I made our way to Savanna la Mar without incident. I instructed Filton to find out anything he could about the whereabouts of either Cornishe or his son, and to use any means necessary to do so. And so it was that we ended up at the Shark's Head, where I was assured we'd find information, if any was available.

The man who runs this place is known as Harold. Filton briefed me beforehand on his background. He's a sworn supporter of the Society and one of Cornishe's most trusted servants. Filton did not wish me to attend, but I don't trust him to conduct business on my behalf. He might take the opportunity to warn the Society of my presence.

Harold greeted him as an associate, but showed some suspicion towards me, even though Filton assured him I could be trusted. Still, I sensed the innkeeper held something back.

"There has been some damage done to our cause, friend," said Filton. "Joseph was attacked at his home. And his son has turned. Both are on the run. We need to find them before any further harm comes to either."

Harold peered at me before answering. "Can we speak privately?"

Filton followed his gaze. "This one? He's a friend. A voyager from overseas who has interests that Cornishe wishes to pursue. You can trust him, I assure you."

There was a pause before Harold continued. "I've heard nothing," he said.

I knew he was lying. I could see it on his face. I've done enough lying and seen enough liars to spot the signs.

"Well," Filton replied. "You'll let us know if anything turns up."

"Of course," Harold replied, but he looked deeply suspicious.

We turned to leave and then something caught my eye, quite by chance. I happened to glance at the coat stand in the corner, and there it was. Cornishe's jacket. It was that light blue coat I'd seen him in at the Black Castle Estate. I nudged Filton and nodded towards it. He looked at me and narrowed his eyes. I turned to look back at Harold, and in the moment that it took for us to turn around, he'd pulled out a musket from beneath the bar and steadied it on his shoulder. "Get out," he demanded.

"You don't want to be doing this," I responded. "There's no need for anyone to get hurt. All we ask is that you let us know where they are. We'll handle the rest."

"If you don't get out now, I'll kill the both of you and bury you round the back."

I waited until his attention had flitted from me to Filton and then took my chance. Leaping forward, I was able to surprise him before he had a moment to look back at me. I kicked him in the chest. The gun barrel flew upwards and a shot rang out. Harold was stunned by the attack and this gave me the precious seconds I needed to wrestle the gun from his grasp. I kicked him hard in the groin. He bent forwards in agony and I grasped the back of his head and slammed it to my knee. When I pulled his head back up to look at me, his face was awash with fresh blood and screwed up in pain.

"Lock the door," I shouted to Filton.

As he was doing this, I picked up the gun and thrust it into Harold's temple. He was on his knees in front of me, but showed no fear.

A sudden rage swept over me. Images of the past few months flashed past my eyes. The boy murdered in the voodoo ceremony in Hispaniola. The struggle at Black Castle Estate. Bloodshed at the hospital. But over all of it, my beloved Claire. Her death is a deep wound within me, and it's opened up again every time I'm slowed down by lies and diversions. I confess, dear Melchior, that I couldn't control myself. Unluckily for the unfortunate Harold, there was a box of tools near the doorway to the cellar. Keeping my gun trained on him, I pulled the box towards me. My rage was hot and I didn't hesitate. I grasped the hammer and a long nail. I stood on Harold's hand and told him that if he didn't speak up at once, he'd not be polishing glasses anymore. He spat in my face, a mixture of spittle and blood.

It was a rusty nail but it broke through the flesh in the back of his hand cleanly enough. I hit hard and sharp, driving it through his hand and into the wooden floor beneath.

Perhaps it was pride that prevented him from screaming out. His head sank onto his chest. Now he was on his knees before me, one hand attached to the floor, the other forming a fist. Something about the sight of him made me angrier still. So much blood, so much unnecessary pain. I swung the hammer and it hit him in the side of the head, knocking him sideways. He shook his head vaguely and continued to look down, defying my questioning.

"Filton," I cried. "Another nail please."

There was no response. I looked up to find Filton staring at Harold. It was not so much concern on his face, but rather a kind of awe.

"Filton!"

"Captain Maddern, if he hasn't spoken by now, he won't speak at all," said Filton.

But I no longer cared whether he would speak or not. This cursed country was eating away at my mind. I needed to *see* the suffering. To objectify it, to control it. I glared at Filton and he put his hand in the toolbox and threw a nail over to me. It was bent, so when I knocked it through Harold's other hand it took a few blows to get it to go through straight. This time he did let out a sound, a sick groan, followed by a heave as he vomited onto the wooden floor. The sickness angered me more and I hammered harder, missing the nail completely and smashing the bones of his hands. The crunching satisfied me, the feeling of flesh and bone giving way to anger.

"Captain Maddern, sir."

I looked up at Filton.

"He's passed out, sir. You won't get anything out of him until he comes round."

I threw down the hammer and stood up. "He'll be more willing to talk when he wakes up."

I'm confident we'll get what we need out of him. Once again I have faith that I will return with what you need.

Until then I remain your loyal servant,

Captain James Maddern

❦ 40 ❧

2nd April 1766, Savanna la Mar, Jamaica

Cyrus sauntered across the harbour, trying his best not to betray his nerves. He cursed his father again. How could he, Cyrus, a mulatto, make arrangements for an overseas trip? Who would trust him? His father had been adamant that he could not show his own face in public. Maddern would be looking for them both. Who knew what he'd been telling people? He carried before him the good name of a gentleman from England, Melchior Croll. Cornishe, on the other hand, had never seen eye to eye with the Jamaican establishment. He'd had many run-ins with the authorities over the years. If it weren't for his wealth, he would have been locked up for his refusal to cooperate with their rules and conditions. This revelation came as some surprise to Cyrus, who had always assumed his father was part of the establishment in Jamaica. But no, Cornishe had insisted they were more at risk if he were to show his face. He'd explained that Cyrus would not be recognised as quickly. Slaves and mulattos came and went, and people rarely paid them much attention.

And so, furnished with bills of payment, Cyrus left Leoncico under his father's care and took Rose with him in search of a ship headed to England. He was looking for a vessel on the final leg of its triangular route. Something just arrived from Africa that was ready to set off on its way back to Bristol. All they needed was room for a white man, his faithful dog and his two 'slaves'.

Cyrus was cautious as he asked around for information on any ships scheduled to take to the sea. The important thing was not to draw attention to himself and his mission. So far, he had drawn nothing but blanks. It was time to return to the lodging his father had set up, get a good night's rest and start the search again tomorrow. It was then that they received the good news.

"Yeah, I know of something, as it happens," said a short, skinny cockney who was carrying a load of plantains on his shoulder. "There's a ship heading to Bristol in the morning. Some Teaguelander's boat, it is. Carrying a crew of clunches and bottle-heads. And a few slaves. There'll be room for more. As long as you got some coin to pay for it."

Cyrus looked confused. "Teaguelander?"

"Irishman," said the cockney.

"That's good news. Who do we speak to?"

"I'm going that way meself. Follow me."

Cyrus looked at Rose, who looked dubiously back at him, and he lifted his eyebrows and nodded. Without another word the sailor strode into the gathering gloom, at a pace that had Cyrus striving to keep up and Rose scampering along beside him. The streets were busier now, as the cooling breezes of the night swept the fatigue from the heat-exhausted day. Cyrus forged through the thickening crowd, concerned not to lose their ticket to freedom. For one moment he thought he'd disappeared.

"There," exclaimed Rose.

They charged forward at a faster pace and got within arm's length of him just as he was about to turn a corner into the smaller lanes at the edge of the harbour. This took them straight into a dark alley. As soon as they turned into it, the sailor was swallowed up again into the shadows. Cyrus scanned the alley but it looked as if there was nowhere for him to go. Then he felt a shove from behind and heard a yelp from Rose. He turned, his senses on high alert. But it was too late even for him to respond and by the time he'd clocked his two burly assailants, he was pinned against the wall.

It was the surprise of their attack that gave them the advantage. But two large men were no match for Cyrus's strength, and he was able to wrench his arms free from their grip easily. He found himself surprised once again by his speed of movement. He struck out at the nearest and largest of the two men and saw him fall to the floor from a single blow of his forearm. He was about to do the same with the second, when he noticed what was going on behind them. A figure in the shadows was holding Rose from behind, his left hand gripping her throat, while his right hand held a knife to the delicate point under her chin. His grip on her throat was tight enough that she could not utter a sound. She was in mortal danger from which Cyrus could not defend her. He stopped in his tracks.

"What do you want? We have money."

"Oh, it's not your money we want," said a familiar voice. "It's your life."

Maddern shoved Rose into the alley and stepped forward into a pool of moonlight. Cyrus caught a glimpse of the grin on his face before he felt the heavy blow to the back of his head and all went dark.

❧ 41 ❧

3rd April 1766, The Black Prince, Jamaican Coastline, Caribbean Sea

Cyrus found himself staring along the floor of the cage that had first contained him back in Westmoreland Parish. He knew it by its smell. His olfactory senses were so sharpened now, that he soon became aware of the presence of his father, Rose, and most surprising of all, Leoncico, who was curled protectively around his feet. Cornishe was out cold, lying at the other end of the cage. Rose was sat in another cage that was right next to theirs. She had her arms clasped around her knees. As his vision started to clear, he realised she was staring right at him.

"So you're finally awake," she said.

Cyrus looked around the room in confusion. It was too dark to see much beyond the limits of his cage and if there were walls and ceiling here, he couldn't tell. As he tried to stand up, he realised that the swaying motion that he'd assumed was caused by his swimming head was actually real. The floor was tilting.

"We are at sea," said Rose. "That man has taken us again."

"Maddern."

"Yes." Rose looked annoyed, but also ashamed. Once she'd helped that man. Now she was in a cage, just like Cyrus.

"How long have I been asleep?"

"Maybe four hours."

"Fuck it." Cyrus slammed his fist into the bars. He turned to look at the figure of his father sprawled on the floor. "How did *he* get here? And Leoncico too?"

"That was a challenge." Maddern stepped out of the shadows. "After a little persuasion, your friend Harold told me when to expect Cornishe back at the Shark's Head. I was able to hide out there and surprise him when he returned. Fortunately, I had silver weapons to subdue him. The dog tried to protect him. Very touching. Personally, I would have killed it, but Filton has a way with dogs, it seems, and he managed to mollify it. He persuaded me it might be useful for killing any rats that get on board. I agreed to give it a chance, but if it doesn't do as it's told, I'll have it shot and thrown overboard."

"Where is Filton?" asked Cornishe.

"Ah, you're awake," Maddern replied. "I hope you'll forgive my blunt tactics. I knew you wouldn't come if I asked."

"Did you kill him?"

"My dear man, I'm not in the habit of killing unless I have to. Filton served me well. Not as well as he served you of course, but he played his part. I have no use for him now, so I left him behind. You do inspire loyalty in your followers, I'll give you that."

"You're making a mistake, you know." Cornishe glared at Maddern. "Trying to contain werewolves. It doesn't work."

"These bars are made of silver. I know that won't kill you, but it will weaken you."

"I see. One of Croll's precautions, I suppose."

"It will be enough to restrain you."

"You'd better hope so. Believe me, you don't want two werewolves roaming free on a boat out at sea. That won't end well for anyone."

"I've seen what you're capable of. I respect that strength. But you're ours now. And I'm taking you home."

"I'm not yours, or anybody else's," spat Cyrus. "And it's not my home."

Maddern turned to him. "Not physically, no. But spiritually, perhaps. When you step onto the shores of England, you might realise your connection to that place. You've never left Jamaica, have you? Well. Now begins your real education."

"It's not my home either," said Cornishe. "I've long since left it behind. And I'll leave it behind again. After I've torn Melchior Croll's head from his body. And yours too." He stared straight at Maddern.

Cyrus knew his father wasn't bluffing. But what about Maddern? Did he have the stomach for this, he wondered?

They were about to find out.

❧ 42 ❧

4th April 1766, The Black Prince, Caribbean Sea

Over the course of the next twenty-four hours, Cyrus learned more about the ship. It was manned by a small crew and carried around twenty slaves, who were being taken over to England to sell to rich merchants and landed gentry. There was a growing trend for black servants in the households of the rich and fashionable, but they needed to be well trained and civil, so only the most loyal and diligent were brought back.

Cyrus, Cornishe and Rose occupied cages within a private cabin, overseen by Maddern. During the day Cyrus was let out to help with some of the work. His ankles were linked together by silver chains, so he couldn't run. The trace of silver sapped him of his wolf strength, but left him able to manage standard manual tasks, such as tying ropes and cleaning the deck. Cyrus discovered the negroes were kept in holds around three feet high and two feet wide. The heat in these compartments was overbearing. The slaves were forced to occupy two to each compartment. With only one set of clothes for each slave, the smell of sweat, piss and shit filled his nostrils. There were many more of these holds, which would normally carry slaves on the journey from Africa to the Caribbean. But on this leg of the journey they were being used to house rum, sugar, tobacco, cocoa, and other items of value they'd picked up on the west coast of Africa. Cyrus wondered what it could have been like when all the holds were occupied. How could they have possibly survived in these conditions with so little space and so many people?

Before leaving Jamaica, the ship stopped at a few ports along the coast to pick up other passengers going back to the old country, and to collect letters being sent to family and loved ones back home. As they left their final port of call and set off across the ocean, Cyrus took in the final rays of Jamaican sunshine as it sank below the horizon. This was the only home he'd ever known, and despite the hardships and horrors he'd endured, it felt like he was leaving something significant behind. The heat of the oncoming night embraced him, and only the warm wind that skipped across the bay gave any hint of movement in the heavy evening sky. As he leaned over the side of the ship to look at the reflections in the water, he took in a deep breath, allowing his senses to wallow in what would probably be his last taste of Jamaica.

"You ever travelled by ship?" said a tall, muscular man named Alexander. He and some of the other slaves were sitting by the fo'c'sle, as they took a moment's rest from their labour.

"I was born in Jamaica," said Cyrus. "It's all I've ever known."

"The journey here nearly killed me," said the one named Virgil. "The seas were rough, and the food so bad. Vomit, blood, shit, all across the decks. Many slaves tried to throw themselves off. They would rather die than live like this. But they were stopped by the white men. In the end, I got so sick I just lay down and waited for death, you know."

"We did not know where we were being taken," said another, an old timer with lighter skin. "I thought I was on a journey to the land where the gods punish the wicked."

They heard a shout. One of the crew was calling them for food at the stern of the ship. The slaves stood and shuffled back along the deck.

It was light still, but it would soon fade. Around fifteen crew members were positioned on the deck, watching over the slaves. Placed at the centre of the deck were two large buckets. The slaves were each given a wooden spoon and ordered to queue for their dinner. Cyrus stood waiting and cast his eyes over at Maddern, who was glaring at him. He looked away. How long would this journey take? And how many would survive it?

When it was his turn at the bucket, he peered down into an orangey-greenish sludge that smelled of pulped vegetables. He dipped in his spoon and took a couple of gulps of the thick cold liquid before he was ordered to move on and allow another slave access to the provisions.

The next bucket contained water, itself tinged green, and clouded with the remnants of the food from the previous bucket. He took several spoonfuls of the water, his thirst far greater than his hunger. In fact, he had no appetite for the vegetable pulp at all. Perhaps meat was the only thing that could satisfy him now.

Another group of slaves came forward. Amongst them was Rose, who had also been let out of her cage for work duties. Cyrus caught her eye and nodded to her for reassurance. Her clothes were stained. Such was her dignity that, even in her current reduced state, she still shone like a princess. Her chiselled cheekbones, lithe limbs and shining dark skin drew everyone's attention. Cyrus bit his lip. He could see the lascivious glances of the white crew members. As she passed one of the white men, a young sailor named Wilkins, Cyrus noticed his gaze lingered on her.

Cyrus's face grew hot. He'd always been quick to anger, but ever since the transformation it had come on him quicker still. He had been told by Cornishe that he had far greater strength than a normal human, but in truth he didn't need anyone to tell him that. He could feel it in his bones, in every sinew and fibre of his body. But he had no sense of the limits of this strength, and he was anxious about giving it free rein. The need to keep himself under control appeared more pressing than ever.

Besides, any violence that happened on the ship could be potentially disastrous for the journey. Both he and Cornishe needed to reach their destination, that was certain. And if he couldn't get what he wanted from Croll, he was going to have to take it from his father.

❧ 43 ❧

25th April 1766, The Black Prince, North Atlantic Ocean

They had been twenty days at sea, and the day of the next full moon had arrived. Cyrus had hoped that they might reach shore before it occurred, but they'd been delayed by storms and there was no land in sight.

The moon was due to rise late that night and Cyrus was finding it impossible to settle. He squatted on his haunches, teeth grinding, eyes wide open, pupils darting. Leoncico, lying at his feet, could sense his master's anxiety, letting out an occasional yelp or bark. Cyrus glanced across to Cornishe, who was sat cross-legged, eyes closed, as if in some kind of trance. How many decades had his father been through this? Perhaps it got easier.

In the cage next to them, Rose stood nervously and watched over him. "Stay calm," she said. Cyrus didn't seem to hear her.

When the moon emerged from the clouds, it was Cornishe

who started his transformation first. His eyes were still shut, but his head thrust forward with a jerk and his cheeks started to undulate, as if worms slithered just beneath the surface. Cyrus had time to note all of this, but before he finished his thought, a clawed fist clenched in his stomach and pulled at his intestine, as if trying to wrench out his insides. Leoncico was now on his feet, barking, which woke up Maddern with a jerk. He stood up and stared into their cage, transfixed by what he was witnessing.

"It's happening," he said.

Rose nodded, her breathing short and rapid.

Now in the midst of their transformation, Cornishe and Cyrus emitted grunts and gasps accompanied by the creaking of bones and the stretching of skin. Leoncico had become irrepressible and was on his feet, spinning around the cage. Watching in awe, it was only minutes before Maddern and Rose saw Cyrus and Cornishe completely transformed into their wolf forms. Their aspects terrified Maddern – never had he seen such powerful beasts. Their eyes were burning and their jaws, now extended far beyond their human size, looked like bear traps.

Cyrus was the first to react, springing upwards to try to escape his cage. But his body convulsed against the silver bars of his prison. There was no room to turn around, and he let loose his frustration, snarling as he made more attempts to break free from his confinement.

Cornishe's wolf was more restrained. He stood at full height, a short distance from the bars, and stared directly at Maddern, a controlled hatred filling his eyes. This was even more frightening to Maddern than the livid tantrums of Cyrus. It was as if there was more of the human in Cornishe, as if behind those blue eyes he was somehow calculating his next move.

The noise inside the cabin was fearsome with the howls and barks of Cyrus and Leoncico. Maddern hoped they'd calm down once they realised they couldn't break free of their cage, but it soon became clear their frustration wouldn't be quelled. Above the noise, he heard a knock on the door.

"Who's there?" shouted Maddern, trying to sound composed.

"Are you all right in there, sir?" asked a voice from outside.

"Who is it?" bellowed Maddern.

"Jack Taylor, sir," the crew man replied. "Is everything all right in there?"

"Yes, of course, it's just the dog. He's reacting badly to the storm. Get back to your post."

There was a brief pause from outside. "It sounds like a whole pack of dogs from out here."

"I'll deal with it," said Maddern. "Leave it to me."

"All right, sir."

"Get me out of here," said Rose to Maddern, once the crew man had left.

"You know I can't do that. Anyway, you're probably safer in that cage than anywhere else."

Maddern turned back to the monsters. Cyrus's wolf was now crouched at the foot of the cage, panting hungrily. Leoncico was sat next to him. Cornishe's wolf stood stock still, gazing straight at Maddern.

Maddern regarded the silver bars. How certain was Croll that they'd hold the monsters? The idea of the creatures escaping didn't bear thinking about.

Another knock at the door.

Maddern stomped over and pulled the door open. He expected to find Jack stood in front of the door, and was ready to tell him to fuck off and leave him to manage this. Instead, there was nothing but the rain-hammered night. He peered out further to check there was no one there – and then felt the full weight of a dark force. Someone powerful thrust him back into the room. He fell against the cage, reigniting the rage in Cyrus, who turned abruptly to snap at his fingers. Maddern reacted just in time to avoid losing his digits, and recoiled again, back against the far wall. The sole lantern that lit up the room went out. Maddern scrambled, feeling his way along the wall, desperate to reach the loaded gun that was sitting by his chair.

"Rose, can you reach the lantern?"

No answer from her. But what he heard instead terrified him: the sound of the lock on one of the cages clicking and the cage door creaking open, followed by heavy footsteps stepping out of the cage and onto the cabin floor. Maddern's stomach turned to jelly as he heard a low growl.

Maddern didn't have time to wonder who had let them out of their cage. All he could think about was how he'd reach his gun before the werewolves reached him.

The sound of panting drew closer, along with the smell of wolf fur. He could feel them now, approaching softly, stealthily. He heard a creaking sound, and then a hot breath hit his face. He closed his eyes tightly, gripped his fists and prayed it would be quick.

Jack Taylor decided to swing back to Maddern's cabin. There was something about the tone of Maddern's voice that had bothered him. He cast a look at the door, only to find it ajar. He walked up and pushed it open.

"Sir?" said Jack, peering into the darkness of the cabin, which now appeared entirely silent. Or almost silent. The dogs were clearly still inside here, as he could hear their panting.

And something else.

"Sir?" he said again.

The next instant, all hell broke loose. The ship hit an immense wave, which floored everyone who'd been on their feet. Jack was thrown backwards, sprawling across the deck. He tumbled around in a ball, his feet rolling over his head, and landed next to a couple of his shipmates, who were cleaning the deck. Jack looked up, dazed from his fall.

"What the fuck?" said Dobbin, one of the sailors who'd been manning the ship through the storm.

A roar from behind Jack's left shoulder made his blood freeze. It was such a primal roar that his nerves were shredded on the spot and he couldn't summon the will to turn and face whatever it was that made it. Instead he kept his gaze focused on Dobbin, who was now staring with a look of utter terror, to a space over Jack's right shoulder.

"What is it, Dobbin?" said Jack. "What can you see?"

Dobbin was gesticulating at him, trying to get his words out. He pointed to something behind him, but Jack refused to turn. There was another sharp roar, but still Jack didn't pull his gaze from Dobbin's face, fearing that by beholding his plight it would confirm his worst fears.

The first that Jack knew of the situation was when a fistful of claws the size of daggers struck his head. He fell against the wooden deck, as a cascade of blood obscured his vision. He shook himself and looked back to see the werewolf, towering on its hind legs over Dobbin, who was still waving his arms, as if warding off a fly. The werewolf was fast. It grasped Dobbin's shoulders and sank its teeth into the back of his neck. He must have hit an artery, as blood shot into the air. The werewolf flung back its head and let out a giant howl. And then another beast, larger than the first, charged past and landed on the deck.

Jack wanted to call out to his fellow sailors, but he couldn't find his voice, and instead was left to watch in mute horror as the werewolf sprang up the boat's mast and, with a snap of its jaws, brought down an unsuspecting crew member who had been tying ropes with his back to the scene, the roar of the wind blocking his ears from what was going on below.

Jack stared in amazement at the second werewolf, and then turned back to see Dobbin being devoured in front of him. And then a third barking and growling came into his earshot, and he watched as Leoncico, the giant Spanish hound, dashed onto the deck, joining Cyrus in tearing into Dobbin's carcass. The two feasted, while the other werewolf landed its prey and set about tearing chunks out of the body.

The storm was rising in intensity. Captain Maddern was nowhere to be found, and in his absence, one of the more experienced crewmen, a stocky fellow known as Bill by his colleagues, had taken to the deck and ordered his men to secure the ship and tackle the storm. The wind whipped around them as they worked, rain lashing their faces like a cat o' nine tails.

Bill was walking aft to check the anchors when he heard it. A howl that emerged from the storm. It couldn't have been the wind, surely? He stopped and turned his head, then cast his eyes around the ship. He could barely see the space in front of him due to the driving rain. Had he imagined it? He could have sworn he heard something. But no, he realised, it must be the wind, which even now was picking up. He was about to go back to his job with the anchor when he saw a body flying over the side of the boat, as if it had been tossed by a giant. He dropped the rope he'd picked up and ran to the edge of the boat. Was that one of his men? He peered into the rain-lashed darkness. There it was. The body of a man being battered by the waves. But as he strained to see through the rain, he realised the true horror of the situation. The body was headless, severed at the neck. It danced like a scarecrow in the water, waving its loose arms in a macabre warning.

Bill squinted and shielded his eyes, to be sure he was seeing right. The body dipped beneath the waves and was tossed around, and again he got the distinct impression that it was a headless corpse. And then it came up again, but this time in the mouth of a gigantic sea monster. The boats were often followed by sharks, due to the stench of death that emanated from the slave holds, and maybe because of the fact that they sensed that a slave might go overboard. This was one of the largest Bill had ever seen, maybe fifteen feet in total. It had bitten right through the man's stomach and was blindly chomping down into the innards.

Bill turned to shout instructions to the crew, only to face the charge of another kind of beast. A giant wolf-like creature was galloping towards him. Acting on the pure instinct he'd learned on the whaling boats, Bill swivelled backwards a good few feet, leaving an open space where he'd once stood. The werewolf hadn't anticipated the move, and such was its momentum that it couldn't hold itself back in any case. Its great weight crashed against the side of the boat and tore through the woodwork. The werewolf tipped over the side and plummeted overboard, swinging its enormous arms as it fell into the churning ocean. Bill stared on in awe.

The werewolf hit the surface and descended rapidly beneath the waves, like an arrow penetrating a cloud. A large mastiff bounded up to the side of the ship, and stood at the place where its master had fallen into the sea, barking and whining furiously, as if calling to his master to emerge from the depths. It was one of those still, yawning chasms of time, where everything seemed to dim to quietness and darkness.

The spell was broken when the surface of the water thrust upwards in a great explosion, driven by the charge of the shark, but this time with the werewolf wrapped around its snout. The werewolf's arms encompassed the shark's muzzle, its teeth snapping at the snout, its claws tearing at the shark's eyes. The shark was stunned to have discovered itself so quickly turned from hunter to prey, and was thrashing wildly in an attempt to loosen the werewolf's grip. But its hold was too strong and, as they fell back into the ocean, it looked like the werewolf had the upper hand.

Bill now noticed two fins that surfaced about fifty feet from the boat, speeding towards the place where the first shark had submerged. He wondered whether the wolf creature could possibly survive against a school of sharks, when it burst to the surface and swam towards the boat. The fins were moving at incredible speed, and Bill was sure they would catch the werewolf. But just as they neared, it dug its claws into the wooden hull, pulling itself up the side of the boat and springing onto the deck. At the same moment, the two sharks leapt from the sea, with both ends of the slaughtered shark in their mouths, tearing it in two as they pulled in opposite directions, before plunging back into the depths.

The werewolf bounded straight past Bill towards the centre of the deck, where more sailors were emerging after calls for help from their shipmates. As the ship's crew peered into the stormy night, trying to make sense of the mayhem that was happening around them, the werewolf tore into the crowd, felling two men at one blow. It stood over them, pinning the crew member's chest to the boat's deck as it sunk its teeth into the fellow's throat. The men surrounding him backed off, grasping the general sense of danger without being at all clear about the nature of their attacker. At first they thought it must be the mastiff, gone mad with the storm, but then the dog bounded out of the shadows, barking in support of the frenzied attack. In the darkness and rain, all the crew could see were the snapping teeth and spraying blood as the werewolf tore into its victim's prone carcass.

Those few who registered what was going on found the urge to take flight tempered by the horrifying realisation that there was nowhere to run. They fixed their eyes on the beast, and prayed his attention wouldn't turn their way. What they didn't take into account, until it was too late, was the heavy panting sound that emerged from behind them. The one who was quickest to retreat, and therefore the furthest towards the back of the group, realised his mistake first. He bumped into something solid behind him, and turned to discover the immense jaws of a second large werewolf, poised just above his head. Before he could let forth his scream, the monster's teeth clamped down onto his shoulder, ripping through the jugular and sending a jet of blood arcing across the ship's deck.

Cornishe's werewolf stepped over the drained body of its victim. The noise of the storm and the screams of Cyrus's victim had confused the sailors, and before they could react, Cornishe had downed two of them with savage blows to the skulls. The third fell to the floor and cowered in horror. The werewolf sank its claws into the side of his head and snapped his neck.

Cyrus, Cornishe and Leoncico hungrily devoured their victims on the storm-lashed deck of the ship and howled at the full moon that watched over the violent sea.

✻ 44 ✺

25th April 1766, The Black Prince, North Atlantic Ocean

To Dr Melchior Croll, Bristol, England
    From Captain James Maddern

I have barely enough time to record this evening's events so I will write in haste.

An unidentified intruder attacked me in my cabin. Water crashed in and knocked me to the floor. I lifted my head in confusion, spat out the salty spray and turned to the were-wolves' cages. My heart sank. They were empty, the doors flapping in the wind that now bellowed through the room. The monsters had escaped. Fortunately, the girl Rose remained locked up.

I hunted frantically for my weapon. The gun was gone. I had to get to the harpoons below. I waded through the sea water that continued to flood in, and made my way out onto the deck. The winds were fiercer than any I'd seen, but beyond the howling of the wind I could hear something bestial in the darkness. The rain hit my face like a shovel. I groped around the main cabin and moved cautiously towards the sound of the beasts ahead.

As I edged around the outside of the cabin, the extent of the devastation hit me. One of the werewolves, whom I recognised as Cyrus, was feasting on the flesh of one of my dead shipmates. A few more corpses were scattered across the deck. The other werewolf, Cornishe, was leaping up the mast to grab those who'd taken refuge up there. A few shots were fired, but they either missed their target, or were brushed off by the werewolves, who seemed impervious to anything thrown at them by the ship's crew.

Across the deck were the steps that led down to the galleys below. The werewolves were distracted. If I didn't go now, I'd miss my moment. I took a deep breath and then plunged head-long across the deck. I was a few feet from the steps when I looked up to see the werewolf on the mast glowering in my direction. I had seconds to get to the steps and bolt the door behind me. I charged forward and an instant later the were-wolf did the same. The werewolf was faster. It got to within an arm's length of me, and I had maybe three feet to go before I reached the stairs. The werewolf tensed its muscles and prepared to spring. Just as its haunches straightened into a leap, a heavy wooden object swung into the werewolf's head, sending it clattering to the deck.

I was amazed and gratified to see Bill, one of my crewmen, standing on the deck, a large pole gripped in both his hands. He prepared himself for another attack, shouting to me through the storm, "Go!"

I didn't need further prompting, and took to the stairs, diving through the opening. I turned to close the hatch and caught a glimpse of the werewolf as it picked itself up from the deck and shook its head in anger, baring its teeth and preparing to strike again.

The boat lurched violently and I could barely keep my balance as I staggered through the narrow walkways under the deck. I could hear the slaves buried deep in the ship, muttering and wailing. I came across a group of about ten of them, cowering in their bunks.

"Come, we have to work together to allay this attack," I told them.

They were scared but they followed me. On the way past the stockroom, I managed to salvage a couple of harpoon guns, which I held on to for my own use.

"This way," I said, taking them back the way I'd come down. We climbed the steps back to the ship's deck. It was strewn with corpses, most of them in various states of dismemberment. A heavy object rolled across the floor and hit my feet, and I was sickened to discover it was the head of one of the crew. The source of the danger wasn't clear to the slaves, who struggled to comprehend what had caused this mayhem.

"Come on, every one of you must fight!" I shouted. "Either that, or we're all going to hell."

Before they had a chance to realise what they were fighting, the werewolf that was Cyrus landed amongst us from above, taking out three or four slaves in one fell swoop. The others shrieked and fell backwards, but with no weapons they had no chance, and were quickly torn apart. A couple of the braver ones tried to rush the creature, but they were rushing to their doom and fell away just as quickly. We had no choice but to confront the monster. I commanded them to run onto it, hoping the weight of numbers would slow it down. It was still throwing bodies across the deck, clawing its way through, when I took up the harpoon and fired it at the werewolf's shoulder, trying to wound rather than kill it. It was already dazed, and this was enough to send it reeling backwards to the edge of the boat. The slaves were quick to take the initiative and all descended on the werewolf, pushing it further back until they had it pinned against the side rails.

"Careful," I said. "We need to contain it."

"Contain it?" shouted one of the men, as he fought with the others to keep the werewolf under control. "We can't have these animals on the ship, whatever the fuck they are!"

The beast let out a roar of frustration and barged its attackers away. Some fell against the deck, a couple of them into the sea. The creature roared again and yanked the harpoon from its shoulder, then bounded away into the night.

I was frozen in shock for a few seconds. And then something whined in my ear. We all turned to look for the source of the sound. There it was again. A canine whimpering, with an occasional yelp of distress. It was coming from the main deck of the ship. I held up my hand to halt them and crept forward towards the sound, my harpoons held aloft in case the monster sprang from the shadows. I realised the sound was coming from the great gun behind the foremast.

The others stayed behind while I went ahead to investigate. I brandished my harpoons, one in each hand, and side-stepped towards the sound. As I drew closer I could clearly hear the sound of a beast. But it sounded more like a beast in distress than an aggressor. Perhaps it was wounded? I paused, anticipating the confrontation. Then, thinking I could surprise it, I sprang forward, harpoons ready to fire.

There, crouched low to the ground, was Leoncico, Cyrus's hound. It was licking its paw, which was damaged and bloody. I lowered my weapon.

"It's fine," I said, turning to look at the others. "It's just a—"

It was then that the other werewolf attacked. All I saw was a blur of fury as the monster felled three of the slaves in one bound. The werewolf snapped one of their necks, tore a hole through the chest of another, and finished the third by grabbing his throat and squeezing the breath from him.

I raised my harpoons. If I was to go down now, it would be with honour and courage in my heart. My eyes met the eyes of the werewolf and I felt a strange stirring in my soul. I wondered when it might pounce, and girded myself for the final encounter. But the beast didn't move. Something prevented it from attacking me. Still our eyes were locked together. And then I heard a bark from beside me. I turned to see Leoncico standing beside me, but the bark was aimed at the werewolf. The monster bared its teeth, but seemed calmed by the hound.

The werewolf jumped up from its position of attack and bounded straight at me, and then past me towards the front of the ship's deck, with Leoncico in hot pursuit. At that precise moment, the moon slid behind a cloud and darkness descended on the ship like a wizard's cloak.

I looked back across the ship. So many dead and wounded. And then a shout from aft.

"Any sign up there?"

Out of the darkness came the group of crewmen we'd split from earlier this dreadful evening. One of them looked down at the fallen bodies. "Jesus, Mary mother of god," he said in a thick Irish accent. "Did you see it?"

I nodded. "Looked it in the eye."

"And it didn't kill you? You must have some powerful protection."

I turned to look at the mayhem left by the monster. Just a handful of us were left.

"It's still roaming, then," said the Irishman. "There's no killing such creatures."

"Then we must hide until the night is over," I said.

I brought the survivors, a handful of crewmen, down into the depths of the Black Prince and into my quarters. I barricaded the door with barrels of rum and commanded them to lie down where they could and keep silent. There are enough bodies out there for the beasts to feed on. If they don't know of our presence down here, they won't come looking for us.

I am taking these precious moments to write this account. God willing, I will have something left out of this chaos to bring you when we reach Bristol.

Until then, I remain your loyal servant,

Captain James Maddern

❊ 45 ❊

25th April 1766, The Black Prince, North Atlantic Ocean

The men huddled together in Maddern's quarters. These were mostly hardened seamen, but they shivered like children. Every now and then they heard a crash above them; the snarling of beasts and the screaming of men. Their faces grew pale.

Maddern finished his last letter to Melchior Croll, an account of the evening up to this moment. Despite the night's events, he refused to believe their cause was lost. He carefully rolled the letter and placed it into an offshore bag, along with some of his clothes, a compass and purse.

He turned to the men who were cowering on the floor. "Stay here."

"You're insane if you go out there," said Bill.

"You'll be safe in here," replied Maddern. "Don't move and they won't discover you." He opened the door to leave.

Bill followed him out and stood next to him in the space outside his cabin. "Where are you going?" he whispered.

"When the moon sets, the beasts will return to their human form. Then they'll take control of the ship. I want you to help them. Let them bring it into shore. We're hours from the Bristol coast, so you'll be back on dry land by midday tomorrow."

"What about you?"

"There are two lifeboats. I'll take one to shore."

"You won't stay with us?"

"I can't afford to stay. They will punish me if they find me. You can tell them you were just following orders, but I have no excuse. My best chance of recapturing them is to get ashore first and prepare for their arrival. I want you to report that you saw me go overboard. That way they won't suspect that I'll be waiting for them."

"You'll have to get past them first."

"I'll take my chances. You'll be fine. Stay down here until the moon sets."

He slipped along the narrow corridor and made his way back up to the deck. It was eerily quiet, but he knew the danger was still close. He picked his way around the bodies strewn across the deck and reached his cabin. In the darkness he could see Rose, still secured in her cage. She squatted there, looking strangely calm, her face portraying an inner strength. Maddern put his finger to his lips, indicating for her to remain quiet, then unlocked her cage and grabbed her arm.

"You're coming with me."

V

❧ 46 ❧

26th April 1766, Bristol Harbour, England

Cornishe had taken control of the situation on the Black Prince, the minute he'd returned to his human state. Bill did exactly as Maddern instructed him, telling Cornishe there had been a violent attack by unknown aggressors, and Maddern had gone overboard in the melee. He said he would pilot them to the Bristol coast, and after that, he'd have nothing more to do with the ship.

Cyrus was forced to look to his father for leadership, at least until they reached their destination. The crew had been decimated by the events of the previous night, but it was the disappearance of Rose that affected Cyrus most. He couldn't bear the thought that she might have died by his hand. He wondered who had freed him and his father from the cage. Could Rose have somehow escaped and let them out just as they were turning? Did she pay the price for that with her own life?

Eventually they reached the west coast of England. The sight of land had a magical effect on the remaining crew. Still, it took every bit of the strength they had left in them to bring the ship into the harbour.

A harbour official stood waiting to receive them as they shored up. "What happened here then?" he said, when he caught sight of the exhausted men.

"It is a long and sorry tale," said Cornishe.

"I'll need a report. Perhaps you'd like to give it over a pie and ale?"

"That would be most welcome."

"What will you do with these men? They look hardly fit to tie their own shoes. Apart from this one." He nodded to Cyrus, who stood with Leoncico by his side, looking as strong as ever.

"He stays with me," said Cornishe. "The others need assistance."

"I'm sure we can find something," said the official. "Have them wait here and we'll bring them some gruel."

"They need more than that. The journey has taken a heavy toll."

"Well, they can stay in our office for a short while."

"Thank you," said Cornishe. "Cyrus, you'll accompany me to the inn. I'll explain to the landlord."

Cyrus nodded resentfully. He'd begun to hope that landing in Bristol would mark the beginning of his freedom. But it occurred to him now that he would be more in bondage here than he was in Jamaica. This land was completely alien to him. The air was cold and damp, and heavy clouds cloaked the sun. A layer of smoke darkened the sky as far as he could see. He looked around to see rows of tall buildings ascending the banks beside the harbour, solid structures of stone and glass crowded together in a way he'd not seen in even the busiest areas of Savanna la Mar.

Cornishe, Cyrus, Leoncico and the harbour official walked to the centre of town. All around him was every shade of human existence. There were refined ladies and rich gentlemen, ragged white beggars and liveried black servants. He'd never before seen black people looking so neatly dressed. What struck him immediately was the busyness of them all. He'd seen and experienced proper toil in Jamaica, in horrific conditions, but there it was all focused on practical outcomes – the production and distribution of sugar, tobacco, rum. Here it appeared everyone was running around at great speed to no particular end. There was loud chatter, shouts in the street, and an overall sense of urgency, as if whatever they were doing must be done before it was too late. But too late for what?

A group of children stopped and stared at him. No doubt most black people they saw didn't look as rough as he was looking, especially after his weeks at sea. He curled back his lips and bared his teeth like a dog, and they screamed and ran back to their mother. He smiled to himself as he saw them pointing in his direction, while their mother ushered them away with her, as if even by looking at him they were risking damnation.

At the tavern Cornishe told him to wait alone outside, and Cyrus felt a shame that he'd never experienced in all his time on the plantations in Jamaica. It was approaching midday and the city was getting busier with every minute that passed. The smells were foreign to him. He could smell the sewage running near the docks and the horse dung and dog turds that littered the roads. He could smell the rats and the rum, but also the flowers of the flower girls and the perfumes that wafted from the shops nearby. These new sensations almost overwhelmed him, at the same time pumping him with curiosity and an urgent desire to explore.

As he stood conspicuously by the inn, wondering how to conceal himself, something in the corner of his eye leapt to the forefront of his attention. He looked around to see a man, a hundred yards across the road, of sombre disposition, with faded black clothing and an enormous hat that seemed somehow apologetic. He was staring at Cyrus with a look that might have been taken as condescending, except that it also shone with the light of compassion. As their eyes met, the man walked slowly and deliberately towards him until he stood right in front of him. Leoncico let out a low growl.

"Do you speak English?" asked the man.

"I've spoken English all my life," said Cyrus.

The quality of his speech evidently surprised the gentleman. "Then you must come to our church. It welcomes you. And all your kind."

"My kind?"

"You are all God's children in the eyes of the church."

He handed Cyrus a leaflet that announced a public sermon by the Methodist Church, Bristol, on the coming Sabbath.

"I'll do what I can," said Cyrus.

"We await you." The gentleman strode on, his sombre expression unchanging as he made his way down the road.

Cornishe emerged seconds later. "I've secured a room for the both of us."

"I'm to enter as your slave?"

"And how else would I explain you?"

Cyrus scowled and followed him in. "They'd better be good with dogs," he said, scratching Leoncico's ears.

❧ 47 ❧

Melchior Croll awoke from his afternoon nap in a dark mood. Ever since Lil died, he'd found it hard to concentrate. Not that he'd held any sentiment for her. Hers was a cheap life. The world wouldn't miss her. *He* wouldn't miss her. But the research would be slowed immeasurably. She'd been a compliant subject, happy to believe everything he'd told her about her prospects, greedy for the immortality he'd promised. Now she was gone, he was back to square one. Finding another like her, a willing participant, would be difficult.

Meanwhile, he'd heard nothing from his agent abroad. Just one letter that told him he'd arrived in the West Indies, and that was it. Had he discovered anything? Was he even still alive?

He was just about to ring the bell for his manservant when he heard a knock at his door.

"Sir, there is someone to see you," said a voice from outside his room.

"At this hour? Tell them to come back in the evening."

"I don't think you will want to turn away this visitor, sir."

The door swung open. Standing in the doorway was Captain James Maddern, accompanied by a young negro woman. He looked sick, depleted, drawn. Barely alive.

"Dr Croll. I'm back. And I have what you need."

❧ 48 ❧

2nd May 1766, Queen Square, Bristol, England

Cornishe had paid for a week's stay at the inn, giving them a place to settle while they worked out their next move. But before they could formulate any plans, Cornishe and Cyrus had two more full moons to contend with, which meant finding somewhere to shift without drawing attention to themselves. Cornishe told Cyrus the best option was to decamp, along with Leoncico, to the woods around Avon Gorge. They roamed for two days at leisure, the wildlife there providing ample nourishment.

Then there was the small matter of Cyrus's task. He planned to take his father's life, and only had one more shift, during the next full moon, before that option was gone and he'd remain a werewolf forever. But he was struggling with the implications. How did one kill one's own father? Especially a father as powerful and commanding as Cornishe? Cyrus persuaded himself he was looking for the right opportunity, but he was prevaricating and he knew it.

Meanwhile, Joseph Cornishe was making plans of his own. "Once we've accomplished our mission here we'll need to get back to Jamaica," he told Cyrus. "I must get word to Filton. He'll be back at Black Castle by now."

That night, Cyrus awoke in darkness. He sniffed the air and felt a disturbance. Was it because this place was still so foreign to him? Or was there something amiss? Whatever it was, Joseph Cornishe seemed to be sleeping soundly through it.

While his father had past experience of this land, every new sight, sound and taste was novel to Cyrus. He could hear sounds outside, the source of the disturbance. He peered out onto the street. Voices, muffled. Heavy footsteps. His senses were on high alert, triggered by some inner warning, a sense of danger.

He looked down to see the door to the inn below him open. He recognised the shape and stance of the landlord. Someone stepped out of the shadows of the night and leant forward to talk to him. He saw the landlord point upwards, to the room that he and Cornishe were staying in.

Cyrus rushed to his father's bed. "Wake up," he hissed. "We're under attack."

No response. Cyrus cursed and strode back to the bed, ripping the sheets back.

Empty!

His first thought was that his father was the betrayer. But that made no sense. Perhaps he'd simply gone for a night wander and—

Shouting from below.

Cyrus ran back to the window to behold his father holding a man in a headlock, while five others surrounded them. They were attempting to talk Cornishe down before he cut his antagonist's throat. Cyrus could now clearly identify these as armed guards, either military men or private soldiers. They'd all drawn their weapons. The innkeeper, who was standing behind Cornishe, pulled a stiletto knife and was poised to attack.

"No!" Cyrus shouted, instinctively.

Everyone looked up to the window.

Cornishe shouted back up to him: "Run, Cyrus!"

But Cyrus watched in awe as his father snapped the neck of the man he held and tossed his body aside, then ran up the street, three of the soldiers on his tail. The two that remained looked up at his room. One of them broke off and stormed through the entrance. The other stayed put and kept watch.

Cyrus cast around the room. He could hear the soldier mounting the stairs in great strides. He could stand and fight. But there was something about staying, a feeling of being trapped, that drove him. He pulled open the window and leapt to the street below. The soldier who'd waited there was unprepared. A leap from that height would have broken the legs of most normal men, but Cyrus bounced to his feet and struck out at the soldier, all within one movement. His victim was a heavy man, with a round belly, long beard and dirty hair Cyrus's strength was enough to propel him back into the street. He hit the wall so hard that the bone in his shoulder crunched, and he groaned in pain and slid to the floor. By now his other pursuer had reached the bedroom and witnessed the attack from the window. Cyrus darted off, in the direction Cornishe had run.

He followed the sounds of shouting and footsteps that echoed down the otherwise silent streets.

"He's here," said one.

"Got him," said another.

He scanned the harbour, spotting Cornishe. His father had

reached the end of a short pier, his back against the sea. He stood, defiant, to face those who pursued him, and a minute or so later three men arrived, swords drawn, advancing towards him.

Cyrus found himself urging his father to escape. *Jump into the sea. They won't follow you.* But Cornishe stood still, as if he were about to surrender.

Cyrus must have been one thousand yards away, and hidden in shadows, but he distinctly saw his father turn his head and look directly at him, and then back at the men who were poised to attack. The way he held himself, it was clear he was inviting them, as if he'd made the decision that this was the way it had to be. He knelt on the ground, his head held upwards, and placed his wrists together, offering to be secured. The guards came forward, more confident now. They tied his hands together and dragged him to his feet, drawing him away and back into the night.

Cyrus roared his frustration.

If they killed Cornishe, he'd lose his chance to free himself from the curse. It had to be by Cyrus's own hand.

But there was something else. He felt a concern for his father. Seeing him captured, it felt like a loss.

He turned to find his way back when a fist hit him squarely in the chest, hard enough to knock him onto his backside.

A tall, dark shadow stood over him.

"What the hell?" said Cyrus.

He saw through the darkness the outline of a face framed by long straight hair tied back in a ponytail.

"Arawak?"

"Come with me. We don't have much time."

∼

Cyrus sat facing Arawak. "So you were aboard the Black Prince?"

"As a stowaway, yes. There were plenty of places to hide."

Cyrus's eyes widened. "It was you that let us out of the cage! And you say you're a member of the Wolf Society that protects my father? I still don't understand why you didn't tell me this before."

"Your father swore me to secrecy."

"But if you were there to protect him, why didn't you enlist my help?"

Arawak gave him a stern, almost exasperated glare. "I wasn't there to protect him. I was there to protect you."

Cyrus looked even more confused.

"He only ever did what he did out of love for you," said Arawak. "Everything was for your benefit."

Cyrus's head swam. No, this was lies. Nothing could convince him that his father had anything but loathing for him. "You believe what you need to believe. I know what my father thinks."

Arawak shook his head. "There's no time for discussion. We must get to him."

"On that we can agree," said Cyrus. If Croll or anyone else killed him, it would leave Cyrus a werewolf forever.

"So how are we going to find him?" Cyrus asked.

"We find Melchior Croll."

"In the meantime, we need to find a place to stay."

"Don't worry about that. Just follow me."

❧ 49 ❧

2nd May 1766, Queen Square, Bristol, England

Cyrus had read much about the European world, but nothing had prepared him for the weather. It was supposedly spring-time, but the air held a coolness that he'd rarely experienced in the West Indies. What the English were calling 'warm' was a cold day where he came from. And it was spoiled by persistent rain. Not the rain he knew, where short, torrential downpours cooled the streets. This was an insidious wetness: slow, steady, unrelenting. He wondered if it always rained like this in England.

And then there was the colour of the sky. A grey, opaque cloudiness blurred out the sun, which sat in the heavens like a burned-out lamp in the fog. A purple tinge lined the horizon and then bled into an iron sky. To Cyrus it felt like the air was heavier here, burdened by its moisture and damning the city like a tomb stone.

It was through this dank air that Arawak led Cyrus. They'd

skirted the harbour, past the rows of ships just landed from foreign shores, alongside those preparing to journey out once more on the triangle of trade. They found themselves in a remote part of the docks, and Cyrus experienced a new form of alienation. Nothing but white faces peered up at them now, happy to stare at the exotic strangers with skin burnished by the sun. Below the fascination Cyrus sensed different emotions – a degree of wonder from some, from others, disgust. Only the shipmen ignored them. These fellows had clearly seen all manner of climes, their own skins reddened by brighter skies. They'd seen other kinds of humans too, and showed no surprise at the sight of others unlike themselves.

After ten minutes of walking beyond the busiest part of the docks, they reached a large warehouse building far from the bustle of the harbour. Cyrus looked around, wondering why they'd come here. Arawak held up his hand, indicating for Cyrus to remain on guard, and disappeared through the warehouse door and into the interior. After a few minutes, he emerged with a quickened stride and beckoned Cyrus to join him.

Cyrus followed Arawak into the warehouse. Lining the walls were groups of huddled paupers. Families, children, babies.

"We can stay here for a while," said Arawak.

"I don't understand," replied Cyrus. "Who runs this place?"

"The church," said a voice from behind him. Cyrus turned to face a familiar figure. The gentleman who'd approached him the day before was dressed in the plainest clothes, but held himself in a pious way, assured of his own salvation. "We are the Methodists of Bristol, and I am the minister," he continued. "You'll be safe here. Just find yourself a place where you can settle down. We can talk about terms later."

"Terms?" said Cyrus.

The minister smiled now. "Please don't be worried. We only ask that you help our mission."

"And what is your mission?"

"To save."

Cyrus nodded in response. "Well, I'm all for saving."

"Then come this way. You must be hungry."

12th May 1766, Bristol, England

The Methodists looked after them well while they continued to make enquiries. They even embraced Leoncico, despite his fearsome appearance. The following day, Arawak came to Cyrus with a tip-off. Leaving Leoncico with some of the beggars at the Methodist mission who had befriended him, they made their way to a coffee house in town. It was pressed with people from all backgrounds and walks of life. Cyrus had never seen so many in one place. He overheard snatches of conversation: investments in sugar, ships sunk in the Mediterranean, slaves overboard off the African coast. Chit-chat on politics and opium, corrupt officials in London and innocent girls being traded by the docks.

The rage in Cyrus was all-consuming. He wanted to rip out the throats of everyone in the place, to take them apart and devour them. It was his wolf getting closer, but it was mixed in with his humanity, a righteous anger, straining against this degrading city that stole people from their homes and sold them halfway across the world.

Arawak had disappeared for a moment, but in a few minutes he returned with a small white man, delicate in bone structure, his features pointed like a bird's.

"This man says he will help us," said Arawak.

Cyrus nodded at him and the man inclined his head, as if paying homage.

"Samuel Bennett, at your service, sir. You're looking for Croll, I understand." He spoke in a refined West Country accent wholly unfamiliar to Cyrus. "I know where he lives and I can take you to see him."

Cyrus peered at him. "Why would you want to help us?"

"Let's just say that Croll has grievously wronged me." He beckoned for them to follow him into a corner of the coffee house, ordered drinks for all of them, and then fixed his steady gaze on Cyrus. "Croll has made enemies but he has made more friends. Like any self-respecting gentleman, he knows how to play the political game. He's a man of science, and he's used that to his best advantage."

"How so?" asked Cyrus.

"The Full Moon Fellowship. It's not unlike the Royal Society of London in its aims. Research into natural philosophy, shared knowledge resources, members in high places. These people have the power, wealth and influence to get almost anything done."

"Full moon?" Cyrus was struck by the implications.

"It's named for the fact that they meet on the night of the full moon every month. It's a practical device. The natural light from the moon makes it easier to navigate themselves home after the meetings. Similar to the Lunar Club in Birmingham."

Cyrus's eyes narrowed. It was too much of a coincidence for his liking.

"Your friend here tells me that you suspect him of kidnapping?"

"Well it sounds far-fetched, but—"

"Not to me. I wouldn't put any crime past Melchior Croll. He hides his real motives well. Nobody suspects what he's up to. Apart from me. I found out."

"Found out what?"

"Things that would discredit Croll entirely, if his associates and colleagues only knew."

"And you've not told anyone?"

Bennett chuckled bitterly. "Unfortunately, Croll is far better at that kind of game than I. He got wind that I'd discovered him and made it his priority to discredit me first."

"And what did you discover, exactly?"

Bennett paused. Cyrus could see by the twitch in his cheek that something deeply disturbing was flashing through his mind.

"Croll wants more than just wealth and political power. He wants to live forever. I think at one time he may have pursued that goal through ethical means. But after so many years, as his obsession grew, and the realisation that conventional learning was not providing the answers he sought, he turned to more esoteric knowledge. I discovered some evidence of experiments. Disgusting experiments. A girl he keeps in his laboratory." He wiped his hand across his face and shook his head. "I'm sorry, gentlemen, I can't go into it in any detail. I hope you will never see what I saw. As I said, when he realised what I'd discovered, he had my name disgraced. Accusations of inappropriate relations with young boys. They stuck. My career as a doctor came to an end."

Cyrus nodded. What he was learning didn't scare him. He

was pleased to be getting the measure of the man. But it did make him wary.

"We need to get to him by the full moon."

Bennett nodded. "It's when they next meet, as I told you. It might be your best chance. People coming and going. They cover their faces, I don't know why. One of those club rituals."

"How do we get in?"

"First we need to find out where it's being held. I may be able to help with that."

"Hmm," said Arawak. "What do you want in return?"

Bennett took a sip of coffee and placed it on the table in front of him. "I want my daughter back."

❧ 51 ❧

13th May 1766, Queen Square, Bristol, England

Bennett stood in front of the big house in Queen Square. Behind him Cyrus and Arawak stood back, trying not to look conspicuous. Not an easy task given the colour of their skin, and the large ferocious-looking dog that accompanied them. People stared at them, as if they were exhibits in a zoo. Cyrus had never seen behaviour like this in Jamaica, and he was sure Arawak hadn't either. He wanted to run at these spectators, just to see the fear in their faces. But there was too much at stake for them to draw attention to themselves.

According to Bennett, this was the residence of Dr Melchior Croll. The man who had sent his agent to the West Indies to capture his father. The man who had set in motion the train of events that led to Cyrus becoming a monster. The man who had waited patiently for years to secure himself a lycanthrope and was about to use his captive for his own ends.

For Cyrus it meant the end of a journey of sorts. But there

was something else. He had come here to end it. To ensure that his bloodline ended with him. To banish the monster and embrace the human. And then back to his real goal, to embrace his freedom.

And all this led to only one thing. Now that he was getting close to it, it scared him. He needed to make sure that Croll got nothing from Joseph Cornishe. But more than that, he couldn't let Cornishe live. If Cyrus wanted to live the rest of his life as a human and not a monster, his father must die by his hand.

Bennett knocked on the door and awaited a response. Minutes passed and Cyrus wondered if Croll had spotted them approaching and was deliberately avoiding the confrontation. Eventually, the door creaked open and there stood Croll's manservant, dressed in a neat uniform of sober grey and black.

"Good day, Cooper," said Bennett.

Even from where he stood, Cyrus could see that the butler was taken by surprise.

"Mr Bennett," was all he said.

"Dr Croll. Is he home?"

"He is not," said Cooper. "He is away on business for a week, maybe more."

Bennett clenched his teeth. "He'll be back for the Full Moon Club, no doubt. Where are they meeting this time?"

"I am not at liberty to divulge—"

"You see those men behind me?" Bennett nodded back towards Cyrus and Arawak. They stood out like aliens in the genteel square. "They have just arrived here from the West Indies. They would kill and eat you without a second thought."

Cooper took a deep breath.

"You know how desperate I am, Cooper. I won't hesitate to encourage them to hunt you down if you don't help me. Just tell me where he is."

Cooper glanced nervously at Cyrus and Arawak, then back at Bennett. "The club meets at the Church of Lost Souls in Henleaze. I trust you won't divulge how you discovered this."

Bennett fixed him a stare. "When this is all over and Croll lies buried beneath the tombs of Bristol, I'll see to it that you pay for your part in these abominable crimes."

At that he turned and stalked back to Cyrus and Arawak at the side of the square.

52

Croll gazed upon the sprawled body of Joseph Cornishe. He'd used chains of silver to secure him to a stone table more than double his size. This was once a church, but Croll had bought it and converted it into an extension of his laboratory. Still, the shape of the vestibule was intact, and even the stained-glass windows remained in place.

Croll thought of Jesus. Not that Cornishe was anything like the Son of God. But they had one thing in common. They were both immortal. Christ had promised everlasting life to anyone who followed him. But that was a lie. Besides, Croll didn't follow anyone, not even the son of God. He would live forever, but on his terms.

Cornishe had yet to wake up in the three weeks since he'd been captured by Maddern's men and knocked unconscious. It took a potent mixture of henbane, opium, hemlock and mandrake to put him under and keep him subdued, enough to kill a normal man. Cornishe was very much alive, but Croll couldn't afford to have him in a conscious state. There was too much preparation and moving around to be done. Nevertheless, Croll couldn't wait to confront him. He grasped his hostage's face by the cheeks and shook it. "All these years, Joseph, and finally I've got you. When I sent Maddern to the West Indies to investigate rumours of werewolves there, I had no idea it would be you he'd find. Now you will pay dearly for what you did."

"Dr Croll." Captain Maddern stood at the entrance to the church.

Croll noticed he was recovering well. He'd heard the entire story, from Maddern's first discovery of Cornishe in Jamaica, to the point where he had left the ship during the attack of the werewolves. After he reached the shore he'd waited for Cornishe and Cyrus to arrive, and then employed a private militia to intercept them. And thus he was able to hand over Joseph Cornishe directly to Croll.

"Is everything ready?" said Croll.

"Yes, sir." Maddern rubbed his chin. "Where is the ... where is Claire?"

"She is being kept in conditions that will favour her return to life."

"Can I see her?"

"I wouldn't recommend it. Her physical condition isn't what it once was, despite my best efforts. But all that will change. You'll see."

"Are you positive of success?"

Croll looked at him. Maddern had done well, better than Croll had dared hope. But now that he'd played his part, what next? He could kill him now. This part of Bristol was quiet, off the beaten track. The only people who ever came here were members of the Full Moon Club. He could dump the body nearby and no one would know or care. It would be easy to convince people Maddern was already dead, lost at sea.

But no. There was more that Maddern could do for him. In due course he would kill him, yes, but not before he'd finished being of service.

"The occasion is upon us," said Croll, turning back to the prone body of Joseph Cornishe, "but the timing is essential. At the point of transformation, the blood of the shape-shifter is at its most potent. It is at that exact moment, when man and beast exist in total equilibrium, that we must harness its power. We capture it, control it and use it to bring new life to the receiver."

"And Claire is to be the receiver?"

Croll looked up at him. "Eventually, yes. But we need to test it first. This process has never been tried before. If we get it wrong, we may destroy the chance of saving Claire forever. No, we need a live test case. Someone we can trust."

"I'll do it," said Maddern.

Croll had not thought it would be this easy. "Are you sure you're prepared to risk your life for this?"

"If it doesn't work, then I'll perish, correct? I have no need of existence if I can't have Claire. And if it does work, we can bring her back too. We'll be together forever in either case."

Croll pursed his lips. "I cannot argue with that logic."

"It is not logic that drives this decision. I have travelled long and hard for this. I can't just stand by and watch."

"Very well," said Croll. "I will brief you fully on the procedure. The full moon will rise on Saturday. We have three days to prepare. We need to keep this one under guard until then. And you. You must get some rest, my friend. Where is the girl, Rose?"

"She's locked in my chamber. She won't escape again."

"Good. We may need her during the transformation."

"I doubt very much she'll comply."

"Leave that to me," said Croll. He put his arm around Maddern and patted his shoulder. "By the end of the week you will be the first man-made immortal in history."

❧ 53 ❧

24th May 1766, The Church of Lost Souls, Henleaze, Bristol, England

Bennett arranged transport for himself, Cyrus and Arawak to travel out of Bristol to the Church of Lost Souls in Henleaze, with Leoncico in tow. He instructed the driver to pull up their carriage out of sight of the entrance. They would have to improvise a plan for getting into the meeting.

They walked around the outside until they found a hedgerow bordering the graveyard, from which they could see the entrance to the church. It was much darker here than in the city, with nothing but moonlight to light their way. Ahead, they could make out the shadows of people milling around. Behind, they heard the approaching sounds of carriage wheels and horses' hooves, and the excitable conversation of guests. The loyal members of the Full Moon Club were eager to see tonight's presentation.

From inside the church, there was nothing but silence. And then came the thunderous sound of the organ, bellowing out through the doorway and filling the space outside, like some wounded giant. Cyrus knew nothing of western music, apart from what he'd heard at the churches of Savanna la Mar. To him it all sounded the same. Rhythmically conservative patterns of blurred notes, flurrying around as if avoiding the truth of their own existence. A futile gesture of faith through sound.

But this was something different. This he could feel. It sounded like a requiem, a clarion call at the gates of hell.

"They are checking people at the door," said Arawak.

"Yes, I noticed that," Cyrus replied. "We can't just walk in there. What we need is a distraction."

"I can do that," said Bennett.

Cyrus looked surprised. "If Maddern sees you ..."

"No one will see me. You two will be far more effective once you're in there. Just watch out for the moment when the doorman leaves his post and be ready to move in as quick as you can."

Cyrus nodded.

"I will not attempt to gain entrance myself. Do not be concerned. I believe my daughter is being held captive at Croll's house. I'll make my way back there now. Croll won't be returning home until later this evening."

"What will we do once we're in there?"

Bennett reached inside his coat and withdrew a handgun. He held it out for Cyrus.

"I suppose that will help," said Cyrus, taking it from him. "But don't you need it?"

"Don't worry, I have another," said Bennett. "I wish you both the very best fortune."

With that, he strode towards the doorway. They watched as he approached the doorman and began to remonstrate with him. With attendees arriving, this was clearly causing some embarrassment. Bennett became louder and more animated and then struck the doorman on the chest. This triggered a more violent reaction and, during the ensuing scuffle, the doorway was left completely unattended.

"Now's our chance," said Cyrus, shoving the handgun into his pocket. He turned to his dog. "Stay here, Leoncico. We'll be back for you after we've finished our business." Leoncico whined and lay down, his tail thumping against the ground.

While everyone was distracted by the commotion, Cyrus and Arawak ran towards the open doorway and slipped into the church. Once inside, they searched for a place to hide. Cyrus knew that nobody would be expecting a mulatto and a West Indian at this gathering. A cursory look at either of them would arouse suspicion, so they couldn't afford to be spotted. A set of steps next to the doorway led up to the gallery, where the organ was still pounding out its solemn dirge.

Cyrus mounted the steps at speed, with Arawak close beside. When he reached the top, he peered over the platform to check on who might be there. Apart from the organist, who was hidden from view, it was empty. They could stand by the wall between the platform and the organ and they'd be invisible to everyone there. The only danger was that someone else might climb the stairs. Cyrus's senses were on high alert, and he was confident he'd get plenty of warning if they were about to be discovered.

The shouting downstairs quietened. He heard a voice conveying news from outside to someone inside the church. "It was some lunatic claiming we'd stolen his daughter. It's all right, we've got rid of him. He gave this gentleman a nasty knock to the head, though."

"Here, give me a hand to bring him up here, where he can lie down and recover," said another.

Footsteps on the stairway. Cyrus glanced at Arawak and

held his finger to his lips. He could hear two men, who were presumably carrying the stricken man between them. He crept towards the top of the stairway, ready to grab them before they became aware of the two of them. With the element of surprise on their side, they might just get a chance to silence them before the alarm was raised.

Another creek. Heavy steps on the wooden stairs. They were slowed down by the weight of the injured man, but they'd be upon them in a few more seconds. Cyrus and Arawak tensed. If they were going to get caught, they'd go out fighting.

"Wait, I'm fine, I'm fine." This must have been the injured man.

The footsteps stopped.

"Really, I am feeling better already. Please, let me come back down and take a seat. The ceremony will be starting soon and I want to be part of it."

"Are you certain?" said one of the men carrying him.

"Yes, certain. I feel fine, actually. It was a minor blow, nothing more."

"Well, if you're sure."

Footsteps again, this time descending the stairs and moving away from them.

Cyrus glanced at Arawak again and breathed out.

The organ music stopped and below there came a tapping sound from the front of the church.

"Gentlemen," said a deep, sonorous voice. "It is time for the ceremony to begin."

❧ 54 ❧

24th May 1766, The Church of Lost Souls, Henleaze, Bristol, England

Cyrus peered through the curtain, and looked down on the altar. The congregation, if that's what it could be called, was in place. It consisted of around fifty people, all male, all distinguished looking. Clearly a moneyed class; gentlemen with influence and power. Once inside they were all handed masks, like those worn in carnivals and masquerades, which leant a sinister atmosphere to the occasion.

The church echoed with muttering and chattering. And then silence descended, for a reason that Cyrus couldn't make out at first. Then he saw why. A large man with a dark beard and white hair stepped forward onto the podium at the front of the church. He had on the coat of a surgeon. Cyrus had expected Christian vestments. It seemed strange, as if science were forcing itself into this house of God. Cyrus had no religion, but still it struck him as blasphemous.

The speaker addressed the congregation. "It is with a joyful heart that I welcome you today to the Full Moon Club. This is the night we have waited for." He paused and swallowed. "I can't tell you how far back this moment presented itself to my mind. How far back I dared to believe. I can honestly say that it's been the main focus of my life for nearly twenty-five years."

A smattering of applause. With a jolt, Cyrus realised this must be Melchior Croll himself.

"Thank you, thank you." Croll nodded, with a hint of ... humility? Showmanship? "Those who have known me well during that time will surely know how ardently I've pursued the knowledge that now lies before us. It is a knowledge that will take the human race in a new direction. Gentlemen, I present to you ... the greatest find in the history of mankind!"

With this pronouncement he waved his arm in a dramatic gesture towards the area in front of the podium. Cyrus leaned further forward to see. There, before Croll, a body lay strapped to a giant platform.

It was the body of his father, Joseph Cornishe.

"For too long man has sought in vain for sacred knowledge," Croll continued. "He has looked for it in the philosopher's stone, the ark of the covenant, the holy grail. He has travelled to holy lands and embarked on perilous journeys into alien cultures. But here, tonight, before us all, lies true knowledge. Knowledge of the eternal, the secret wisdom of everlasting life. Gentlemen, at the hour of the full moon itself, this human flesh will transform, to become a supernatural form. A lycanthrope, or werewolf. Within the essence of this supernatural hybrid lies the ancient mystery of immortality itself. And tonight I mean to capture that essence, and find a way to use it for the benefit of all mankind. My mission all along has been a simple one. To establish man's place at the head of the cosmos, where gods once sat. To separate man's place from the rank and file of earthly creatures. To lift ourselves from this soil and place us where we belong, above the circle of the moon, with heaven and earth beneath our feet."

His words were having considerable effect on the audience before him. A few cheers were heard, along with random shouts. Some even seemed to be experiencing a kind of religious fervour.

"We have just twenty minutes before the full moon makes its appearance and the ceremony will begin. In the meantime, I am proud to introduce the man responsible for returning this miracle to us. Captain James Maddern will give a short talk on his adventures overseas and the events that led up to the capture of this invaluable prize."

The applause was polite. It seemed nobody had heard of him.

Captain Maddern approached the stage and cleared his throat. "Thank you," he said. "I would like to begin."

Cyrus turned away from Maddern's speech and whispered in Arawak's ear. "We haven't got much time. I don't know what Croll means to do, but it sounds like the moment of transformation is critical to his purpose."

"Then we must free him now," replied Arawak.

"I'm afraid it's too late for that," said Cyrus.

"Too late?"

"The only sure way to avoid Croll taking this power is to destroy his means of doing so."

Arawak looked back at him, a frown of confusion on his face. "I don't understand. You don't mean ..."

"I mean to take Joseph Cornishe's life before he transforms," said Cyrus.

Arawak stood up. "You will not."

"We have no choice," said Cyrus, drawing himself to his full height.

Arawak stared at him. "You're not doing this to protect us

from Croll. This is an agenda that serves your own needs. You want to rid yourself of the gift that you call a curse. To destroy that part of yourself that was given you by your father. And you're willing to kill him to do so."

Cyrus frowned. "You don't understand. To me ... he's not a father."

"He has done everything a father could do for his son. Of that I can be sure."

Cyrus laughed. "Everything? You mean keeping me as a slave since the day of my birth, sending me away from my home to work in a trade I never wanted, refusing to acknowledge my pain? You think that is a father's role?"

"And what else could he do? You are a black man, Cyrus. A black man in a world where black men are slaves."

"I'm half black. I'm also half white. And now I'm only half human, thanks to him."

"Do you realise how far he has gone to protect you in the past? Now it is your turn to do something for him."

Cyrus shook his head. "You must understand. I have to end this. For myself."

Arawak was about to make another protest when Cyrus drew out the handgun and held it aloft.

"I'm sorry, Arawak. This is the end. I need to realise my destiny and find my freedom."

"Don't be foolish. You can't kill him with normal bullets."

"I just need to get close to him. A werewolf can kill another werewolf, correct? The moment I turn, he'll be my first victim."

"What will you do when it's done? Where will you go? You'll be hunted down, enslaved, killed probably."

"I'd rather die as my own man, than live as a slave."

Before Arawak could move towards him, Cyrus vaulted over the balcony and landed at the back of the church. A descent of some twenty feet that felt like a skip over a country stile. He was much stronger now. The strength that the wolf gave him, made more powerful still by the imminence of the full moon. He turned to assess the congregation. Every member of the masked audience faced the stage. Maddern was nearing the end of his speech. Cyrus crouched and ran along the right side of the church, staying well hidden behind the pews, until he came close to the front. Everyone too intent on what was going on in front of them to notice his presence.

"I've seen for myself what these monsters can do," Maddern was saying. "I was eyewitness to a voodoo ceremony of unimaginable horror. This is just the beginning of the war. Once the great Melchior Croll has brought this power under his control, we will see an end to it." He gestured to Cornishe, still unconscious on the altar. "This man was once a gentleman. He had breeding, taste, intelligence. But he was corrupted by this pestilent black culture that pervades the West Indies and the African homeland that feeds it. I foresee a time when we will wage war on these beasts. And when they no longer serve our purpose, we will eradicate them from the world forever."

"But this isn't a black disease, is it?"

The entire congregation turned to look at Cyrus, as he stood in the front row, his gun pointed directly at Maddern.

Maddern stared in shock at the interrupter. "Cyrus!"

"It was the white man that brought this blight to the West Indies," Cyrus said, moving closer to the stage, his weapon trained on Maddern. "Werewolves are not indigenous to Jamaica. The lycanthrope is a European creature. If you want to blame anyone for this monstrous curse, blame yourselves. Blame your desire to dominate nature. Blame your need to put other races of the world under your control, to subjugate humanity itself to the demands of commerce and capital."

"An eloquent speech." Croll had emerged from the shadows at the back of the church and was now standing on the stage. "But you don't know the smallest thing about it, do you, Cyrus? You haven't spent any time studying, researching, experimenting. Your father here was my accomplice once. We were working together to unravel the mystery of eternal life. But in the end, he became selfish. He ran, took his secret with him. And denied me the chance to share in the glory he'd discovered."

"Count yourself lucky," replied Cyrus. "There is nothing glorious in the condition that my father and I are cursed with. I plan to put an end to it, both his misery and mine."

As he said this, Cornishe made a loud gasp, his chest heaving in great gulps of air. At the same instant Cyrus felt a wrench in his stomach that had him doubled over in pain. This was it. The change was coming. The time had finally arrived for him to finish it.

"And now, I'm afraid, we're all out of time," Cyrus continued. "Move away." He pointed the gun at Maddern, who was standing between himself and his father, and pulled back the hammer.

Kill your own father? Is that what you want?

Rose? Her voice was in his head as clear as if her lips were next to his ear. He looked up to see her standing in the shadows at the side of the stage, her wrists bound together. Her eyes were shut tight and her face screwed up in deep concentration. Maddern must have taken her with him when he fled from the ship.

"He's no father to me," said Cyrus, out loud.

You cannot deny your own father. Joseph Cornishe brought you into this world. He may not have been the father you wanted, but you owe him your life.

Cyrus looked down at his father, who at that instant underwent another severe spasm, in synchronisation with the internal shocks that Cyrus was experiencing. These were the last few moments before the change.

"Move out of the way," he said to Maddern. "I need to get to him." He prepared to shoot, his finger tightening on the trigger. From the corner of his eye he saw Croll advance towards Cornishe. He pointed the gun back and forth between Maddern and Croll. "Stop! Or I'll kill you both."

"You're too late," said Melchior Croll. "In fact, not only are you too late. You're surplus to requirements."

Cyrus felt an arm around his neck and the weapon was snatched from his hands. Someone pressed a blade to his throat. It was a blade of pure silver. He could feel its heat burning into his skin.

On the stage, Croll pulled a lancet from the table in front of him. Next to it was a large glass jar, with a tube dangling from it. Cornishe went into another violent fit and Croll plunged the lancet into Cornishe's forearm. Blood flowed like a fountain, splattering onto the floor around them, as Croll hurriedly attached the tube with a cannula to the open wound. Cornishe's blood began to fill the jar.

"Your father will die, of course, and he will die slowly," said Croll. "Once I have taken every ounce of blood from his body, he will be left an empty shell. Not even a werewolf can survive that. And then his secret will be mine. It is what they call 'killing two birds with one stone'." He turned back to look at Cyrus.

And then came the first real jolt of the change.

A burst of energy filled his chest and the wind filled his lungs. His back rippled with the crackling of his wolf spine as it thrust upwards and forced his torso into its wolf shape. He felt the ripping in his arms as the bulkier muscle of his bestial form surged to the surface. Whoever had been holding him was unprepared for the violence of the transformation and, for a fraction of a second, relaxed his grip on Cyrus's body. It was enough for Cyrus to throw back his arms and knock his unknown assailant to the floor.

At that same moment, Cornishe was going through his own change while still bound by the silver chains. His blood was starting to run through the tube at a faster rate now, propelled by the tremendous explosion of Cornishe's transformation.

Despite the change, Cyrus had enough of his human consciousness about him to keep his purpose in focus. He knew from experience that this wouldn't be with him for long. It would only be a matter of minutes before the full wolf brain took over and human consciousness would be lost to him. He had to act fast. His father must die, at his hand. He made his last monumental effort to fight the barbarous fog that descended on his brain and tensed himself to leap and reach the prostrate body of his father. It had to be before the transformation was complete.

He felt the muscles in his legs stretching out like wire and used that cue to propel himself forward. It would only take one or two slashes to his father's throat and he would take the head off his body.

As Cyrus pressed his heel to the floor and felt the familiar bursting pain of claw through skin, he was stopped in his tracks by a nearby voice.

"You don't want to do this."

Rose again. But this time it was spoken out loud.

He whirled around to find her watching him. There was something commanding in her eyes, something he couldn't resist.

"I know you don't want this, Cyrus," she said. "Your father isn't your enemy. You know that too, in your heart."

Cyrus felt his muscles relax at the sight of her. He'd never felt this before. When the change was upon him, there was only one direction it could go. But now it seemed as if he were going back to his human self. Why was she trying to stop him? His shift had been taking him fully into his anger and the rage he had for his father. But the appearance of Rose started some other current inside him. He felt a conflict within his veins, as if the very atoms in his body were split into two, fighting each other for dominance. He wanted to tell her something, something just beyond his understanding, but once again words were losing their meaning to him in the submergence of his logic to the wolf. All that was left was the noise of the beast, the roar that went with it, and the total embrace of his animal core.

Rose focused all her energy towards him. By now his fangs were distended and the fur was starting to crackle through the skin on his arms and chest.

"Stop," she said. She glanced over at Croll, who was distracted by his bloodletting.

Cyrus turned and looked at his father, restrained, mute, vulnerable. It took all of his strength to fight the desire to rip him apart.

Rose glared at Cyrus again. "It is not your father you despise. It is yourself."

Cyrus knew she couldn't stop the change, no one could. But in this pause was a kind of clarity. His senses, heightened by the transformation, now perceived something else about the world. He'd been a man. He'd been a beast. But this was a space between those two states. For the first time in his life he felt ... free.

He leapt up to the stage and towards Rose, grabbed the bonds that tied her wrists and ripped them from her. He tried to yell "Run" but it came out as a twisted roar.

The last vestiges of humanity left him and he let the

torrent of the beast take him. It had a new direction now, echoing from the final thoughts he'd had in his human form. But there were no words for it, just the goal. He turned, struck Croll so that he fell to the floor, and crouched over his father. Their eyes met, and in them Cyrus saw himself. There was no fear there, no hatred, no emotion at all. Just a mutual recognition.

Cyrus extended the claws in his right hand and tore downwards.

But it was not flesh that he tore. It was the chains that kept his father bound to the altar. They did not yield, and the silver of the chains burned his hand. He growled in pain and anger.

"Out of the way," cried Rose.

Despite his surrender to his wolf form, Cyrus heard her voice deep in his consciousness and found himself obeying her instinctively.

The congregation had by now realised that a werewolf was loose. It had taken them a few seconds to grasp that this wasn't part of the plan, but now panic ensued. They surged away from the stage and towards the back of the church.

Cornishe was fully transformed also. He was convulsing against his chains, the silver inflicting a hot agony on him as he struggled against his bondage.

Croll was still prone on the stage and was struggling to get up. Rose had spotted the key chain on his belt and now she tore it from him and thrust the large key into the padlock that held Cornishe's chains in place. It slipped open and the chains fell slack. Cornishe leapt up, his strength instantly restored, and took his place next to Cyrus. Through an unspoken synchronicity, they snarled and turned on their common enemy.

Croll had not expected this. He got to his feet and readied

his silver blade, backing away from the beasts. Maddern cowered behind him, fearful of what his former captives might do.

The werewolves were enormous. Cornishe had the height advantage by a few inches, while Cyrus had heavier muscles. Cornishe's coat was black, like midnight. Cyrus was a dark brown, with hints of red at the edges of his long mane. They could have torn both men apart in an instant, but they were wary of the silver blade. They hunted with their cold blue eyes for a place of entry, a gap to attack.

"So you've come together?" Croll hissed. "Well, it matters not. We have what we came for. I admit I'd wanted to see the end of you tonight, Joseph. For all you did to me, it would have been a fitting finale to take your life. But if not now, the time will come, I am sure of that."

Cornishe snarled. The words had no meaning for him. But he could feel the hatred through which Croll was uttering them. And something primal within him recognised his antagonist.

"The power you have gained is impressive. When you came back to me all those years ago, I had honestly thought we might share this power. But you took the thing I loved and then ran. I swore if I ever found you I'd make you pay. Alas, my revenge will have to wait. But now I have that power for myself at last." He held aloft the glass jar of blood that had been drained from Cornishe. "I have plans for this, plans that will take me further than you can imagine. But you? You can't conceive of that. You're a beast. And even as a man, you could never match my intellect. We will catch up with you again."

Cyrus roared, impatient for the kill.

"Until then—"

Together, Croll and Maddern withdrew towards the back of the church and were swallowed by the shadows. Cornishe and Cyrus bounded after them, but they'd completely disappeared. The frustration in Cyrus could no longer be contained. He turned and leapt off the stage and towards the crowd of acolytes, who had been scrambling to the back of the church. Someone had locked the front doors and there was no other exit. Cornishe joined Cyrus, and both monsters advanced.

They were a few paces from their victims when they stopped dead in their tracks.

In front of them stood Rose. Her arms were stretched out before her, palms facing them, fixing them both with an intense and fearful gaze.

"Hear me Sasabonsam! By the power of Tano's fire, you will stand back!"

Both Cyrus and Cornishe were frozen in place. Their faces betrayed no less fury than before, but they seemed powerless to move beyond an invisible line in front of them.

"Well done, girl," said someone in the crowd. "Now help us get out of here."

Rose held the werewolves in place with the power of Obeah and then turned to the crowd. "I'm sorry to disappoint you, but I am not your saviour. None of you will escape tonight with your lives."

Shrieks from the crowd.

"But, before I commit you to hell, I want you to fully understand why you are condemned. It is for everything you've done to me, my brothers and sisters, and all my people. For the capture and imprisonment, the savage beatings, the vicious rape and brutal torture of innocents. All of this for what? Sugar? Rum? Wealth? You have done a very great wrong. You have sold your soul to the devil to satisfy your appetite and your greed. Tonight it is your turn to pay."

"Please, spare us," cried an elderly gentleman in the crowd. "Tell us what it is you want."

"There is nothing you can give us beyond what you owe us," replied Rose. "You must now pay the price."

"Wait!" said another. "If everyone here dies, there will be consequences. Others will come for you. Why not leave us in peace and go on your way?"

"You are not people of peace. You deserve everything that is coming to you." Rose turned to face the werewolves and flung her arms down. "*Lobos ... destruir!*"

The two werewolves roared past her and into the crowd.

☙ 55 ❧

24th May 1766, The Church of Lost Souls, Henleaze, Bristol, England

For the first time, Cyrus could see through the eyes of his wolf. He had no control. That was in the past, and it would come again. But he could observe. He could feel what it was like to let his wolf take over this body and command its will. It was as if he, the human Cyrus, were in a coach, driven by the devil and pulled by wild horses. During the mayhem he saw through the wolf's vision, a thick green fog, slashed with streaks of red from the spilt blood.

And there was a lot of spilt blood.

He heard the shriek of other people's terror, while his wolf's drive for savage justice ploughed through the crowd, like a scythe through sugar cane.

He felt the easy glide of his claws through human meat. These beings were no longer human, they were swollen bags of flesh. The heat of their blood, the way it flowed around them, circulating through their slow, fatted sacks, their pumped hearts driven by the terror they saw before them, a terror inspired by the werewolf Cyrus, and his father, Joseph Cornishe.

Hunger was there, but it wasn't the driving force. There was something more primal to it, as if this destruction was a realisation of his wolf's being. As if, without it, there would be no wolf. It was the action that made the creature. Cyrus the man was now powerless, an observer. The wolf was the agent. Its essence was conflict, a war against nature itself.

At the same time he was aware of the presence of his father. The two of them were somehow acting in unison, despite the apparent random savagery of their attack. It was a familial bond he had never before experienced. Despite his foggy vision, Cyrus the man would occasionally get a blast of sensation, like the thunderous drums of the slaves during their night revelries on the Black Castle Estate.

There was no escape for the victims. Arawak had secured all exits. Some tried scaling walls, hiding behind pews, rushing to the back of the church in the hope of finding another way out. But it was no stretch at all for the werewolves to catch them like fish in a barrel. Their flesh was so weak that a single swipe across a vital artery would floor them. Within minutes there was nothing but death. Limbs and torsos carved up and laid bare. Occasionally the groaning of a still dazed victim. Cyrus was surprised at how his wolf finished them all off before moving on. Letting a human live would mean another werewolf in the world, and that was something the wolf did not want. Perhaps it was the potential competition.

Finally, there came a pause. Cyrus sensed the wolf was satisfied. Every living creature in the place was dead, aside from Cyrus and Cornishe, and two others who hadn't been attacked.

Arawak and Rose stood quietly at the balcony overlooking

the carnage. Something in Cyrus's wolf wanted to finish them too, he could feel that, but there was a strong signal that he should spare Arawak. The signal came from his father's wolf, he felt, and it had something to do with a bond between them that he didn't fully understand. As for Rose, she had an irresistible power, a magic that exerted complete control over them. There was no touching her.

When all were dead, the werewolves started to feed. The food was bountiful and Cyrus gorged himself into delirium. The night became a haze. Eventually, his wolf relaxed into a comfortable rest and then, finally, sleep.

𝕾 56 𝕾

25th May 1766, The Church of Lost Souls, Henleaze, Bristol, England

Cyrus awoke, surrounded by the dead. Arawak was leaning over him, offering him a drink of water.

"Take," he said, pushing the cup to his lips.

Cyrus gulped it down and cleared this throat. He noticed Rose at the back of the church, got up and walked over to her.

"You saw it," he said. "You were part of it."

"Put on some clothes before you speak to a lady."

He turned and looked around at the victims for clothing he could steal. There was plenty to choose from, but he felt a deep sense of shame at taking the clothes from the dead. Rose moved off, and he bent down and took a pair of golden brown pantaloons and a black shirt from a man who lay close by. He looked over to see that his father had already done the same. Joseph Cornishe looked entirely natural in his clothes, but Cyrus felt absurd in the rich vestments of a wealthy white man. He wished for the outdoor garments that he wore during his time in Jamaica. It hit him then, how much he missed the place. He'd always assumed he was out of place there. But that was before he'd seen anything of the world. In fact, that land where blacks and whites lived together, even if it was in monstrous imbalance, reflected his nature better than the European world in which he now found himself. Whatever freedom he could conceive for himself was overwhelmed by the sense of being trapped in a foreign land, far from home. Strange that he'd never considered Jamaica home before. Only now he wasn't there could he truly see.

Cyrus had fed well last night. This morning, his physical strength was at its peak. But the thought of his homeland and the thousands of miles he'd travelled away from it gave him a heavy feeling in his chest. He heard a sobbing sound and then realised it was coming from himself. The awareness made it worse, and he fell into a heaving, gasping, desperate state. He fell to his knees and cried, for what felt like the first time in his life.

He felt an arm around his shoulder, and looked up to see his father staring at him earnestly.

"We've got to get away from here, as soon as possible," said his father. "The four of us are criminals. It will be difficult to go unnoticed."

Cyrus nodded. "Where can we go?"

"We may find shelter with someone I once knew. I haven't seen her since I left England, but perhaps she will look favourably on us."

"Is it far?"

"Just here in Bristol, presuming she hasn't moved on." Cornishe paused. "And presuming she can forgive me."

Cyrus stood up and held on to his father, so that they were now arm in arm. "Everyone has the capacity to forgive," he said.

❧ 57 ❧

25th May 1766, The Church of Lost Souls, Henleaze, Bristol, England

Cyrus found Leoncico in the woods outside the church, just where he'd left him. The dog leapt up at him and licked his face, tail wagging. The challenge now was to find their way back into Bristol without drawing attention to themselves.

"No easy matter," said Cornishe. "We all have the look of foreigners, and you three look like slaves."

Cyrus might have taken affront at this remark in earlier days. But now he saw in it something new. Cornishe had described them as 'looking like' slaves, not 'being' slaves. Maybe he was overanalysing. But he'd never had anything to hold on to in the past. This would have to do.

"The only thing for it is to split up," Cornishe continued. "I'll take Cyrus with me. Rose can look after Arawak."

Rose nodded. Clearly Cornishe had respect for her power.

"No," said Cyrus. "You go with Arawak. Rose and I can manage more effectively."

Cornishe was about to refuse, but was stopped by the look Cyrus gave him. "You're right. That's sensible. We have two more nights of transformation to get through. If we spent those together it would be difficult to avoid garnering attention. I suggest you return to the woods I took you to at Avon Gorge. Arawak and I will find something similar on the other side of the city, where we can go undiscovered." Cornishe extended his arm and grasped Cyrus's hand. "We will meet at St Mary Redcliffe Church in Bristol, three days from now, at midday precisely. I'll give you directions for that too. In the meantime, take care, my son."

Cyrus nodded, kept hold of his hand a second longer, and then smiled. "You too, Father."

GET AN EXCLUSIVE FREE BOOK

Thank you for reading ABOVE THE CIRCLE OF THE MOON.

I hope you enjoyed it.

I love to keep in touch with my readers, share information about my books and special offers. Sign up to my email newsletter now and you'll get a free copy of THE SHAPES OF BEASTS, the prequel to ABOVE THE CIRCLE OF THE MOON.

THE SHAPES OF BEASTS

Bristol, 1720: Joseph Cornishe discovers his parents brutally murdered in his family home. He leaves everything he knows and rampages across Europe – fighting, drinking and struggling to find a way through his grief. Twenty years later in the Russian wilderness, he stumbles on the one thing he wasn't looking for: true love. But it comes in the shape of the mysterious Elizabeth, who hides a terrible secret. Joseph learns too late that his love is a werewolf. She leaves him, but not before inflicting a transformative bite. Now Cornishe must find his lost love, and conquer the Lycan curse that will change him forever.

Sign up and get your free book here:

https://tmtucker.com

PLEASE LEAVE A REVIEW

If you've enjoyed ABOVE THE CIRCLE OF THE MOON, I would be grateful if you'd leave a review on the book's Amazon page. Honest reviews of my books help bring them to the attention of other potential readers.

ABOUT THE AUTHOR

T.M. Tucker is the author of THE SHAPES OF BEASTS
(available exclusively to email subscribers) and ABOVE THE
CIRCLE OF THE MOON. He is working on Book II of the
Cornishe Chronicles.

For more information:
Web: www.tmtucker.com
Email: tim@tmtucker.com

facebook.com/tmtuckerauthor

twitter.com/tmtuckerauthor

instagram.com/tmtuckerauthor

For more information:

Web: www.tmtucker.com

Email: tim@tmtucker.com

First published in 2020 by 23 Digital Ltd

Cover design by Sarah Whittaker

ACKNOWLEDGMENTS

Bryony Sutherland for her brilliant editing.
Phil Lecomber for his inspiration and feedback.
Andrew Lowe for his advice and encouragement.
Sarah Whittaker for the wonderful cover design.

Printed in Poland
by Amazon Fulfillment
Poland Sp. z o.o., Wrocław

58302226R00171